THE CHRONICLES OF MERWORLD

A PARANORMAL ROMANCE OF SEXUAL ALCHEMY

BY

ELIZABETH MONROY

Print Editions 1.1 2022

ISBN-978-1-958184-29-5

INFINITE HUMAN PRODUCTIONS

www.infinitehuman.com

Enquires: infinitehumanproductions@gmail.com

Infinite Human Productions L.L.C USA, Italy

Table of Contents

PROLOGUE

MerWorld Revealed

There is a secret place within the depths of the sea
Hidden in a cavern, is what a sailor once told me
Protected from the cruelty of the Lander's merciless rage
Lies many a Wise Whale Woman and an Ancient All-Knowing Sage
Sunken in the deep, dark waters and the recesses of the mind
Cast away from the world of light, and hidden from space and time.
There is a world beyond this world, where life is merry and gay
There is a life beyond this life, where Mermaids swim and play.
So come, all ye sailors, when the ocean blows up a gale.
Heed the siren's call and know
That there is truth behind my tale.
Come to the land where MerPeople swim free
Where no sickness or sorrows abound
Come to the place at the bottom of the sea
When your ships have run aground!

"People don't believe in mermaids anymore...sure, you might see their images pasted on the side of a can of tuna fish or a topless bar called The Sexy Sirens or in a children's cartoon. But basically people have stopped believing. In my day everyone believed in mermaids. We not only ruled the sea, but the land and the winds. But those days are gone. Let me tell you what happened. My name is Serena. I was at one time Queen of the Sea."

CHAPTER ONE

"Five hundred feet below the Pacific Ocean's surface, near the Marshall Islands, lies the entryway into an enormous underwater cavern. Cleverly hidden behind huge tendrils of seaweed, coral and algae, and nestled on the ocean floor, rest the glistening bubbled domes of the City of Mer, the bustling center of MerWorld. This underwater city was home to over five thousand Mer People. There were four distinct tribes, or Quams, within the social structure of Mer. Each Quam had very specific rules for living, dying and everything else in between. The Dolphin Quam was a playful, gregarious group who loved social functions and sporting events. Then there was the Turtle Quam: they were the scholars, the teachers and those who kept and recorded MerHistory. The next Quam was that of the Shark. These were the warriors of our culture. Their job was to protect us and hunt for food. Lastly there was the Whale Quam. This was a Quam of spiritual leaders who ruled the other Quams. They were the royals of society and communed directly with the sacred whales. But by my day everything had changed. Our world was already on its way toward destruction, we just didn't realize how rapidly the decline was approaching.

Great chalice-shaped latte stones guarded the outer parameter of the empire while MerWarriors patrolled the dark surrounding waters. Immense, bubble-domed walls held back the vast Pacific Ocean, creating a dry inner sanctum. Each dome-shaped chamber, some forty feet in diameter, linked with another chamber, creating what looked like a great coiled strand of pearls. Spiraling upwards in the center, like a small medieval fortress, sat the Great MerAmphitheater. This enchanting structure was nearly nine hundred feet in diameter and rested at the pinnacle of the coiled bubbled domes. The outer chambers surrounding the Amphitheater made up the palace: my prison.

"Jaween will be joining us for *Growgar*," King Halstaff said quietly in Turtle, as he placed his stubbly webbed hands on Serena's shoulders. Being of the Turtle Quam, he hated to raise his voice. They were a quiet Quam, much more comfortable with the written word. His round bald head and saggy neck showed his age. But the beading eyes that peered out through his turtle-shell rimmed glasses were still alert. He walked awkwardly due to his large belly, which jiggled inside the turtle-shell armor.

"Yes, Father," Serena replied with a courteous Dolphin squeal as she stared back at her dim image reflected within the great mirror, which was spotted, sallow, and partly covered in sea moss. A tarnished reflection revealed the face of a beautiful young woman with a tousled mane of long golden curls that cascaded down her back. She tugged her jewel-encrusted comb through the mass of knotted ringlets. Her golden skin glistened in the fluorescent glow of the plankton lamps. An elegantly low-cut seaweed dress exposed half of a broken emerald heart, which hung between her ample bosoms. The dress was a deep purple, cast with a specially prepared dye from the shells of mollusks and adorned with a geometrical seashell design. Serena raised her head back, exposing piercing blue eyes that flashed with defiance, offsetting the delicacy of her chiseled face. She pursed her lips, holding back her words. Banners of seaweed drapes hung from massive stone columns, strategically positioned throughout her chamber to create both a regal effect and to afford privacy. A striped lionfish, swimming outside the bubble dome wall, stopped to gaze in at the Princess, as if somehow sensing her conversation held significance for the entire kingdom.

Halstaff motioned to Marianna. "See that she looks her best. I expect Jaween intends to initiate the rites of *Kauha*." He waddled his round body toward the door leaving his webbed footprints in the soft, sandy bottom of the Pacific.

Marianna rose and took the inlaid comb from Serena's hand and gently smoothed away the snarls. "Yes, Your Majesty."

A curse on the Shark Quam, Halstaff thought silently as he left his daughter's chambers.

Marianna had dark auburn hair that fell over her mystical sea-green eyes and pale, smooth skin lightly speckled with freckles. She was timid, probably due to the fact that her father was pure Turtle. Her introverted nature made her an outcast among the gregarious Dolphin girls. This was why Halstaff confided more in Marianna than Oceania, Serena's other flamboyant MerMaiden. Marianna's only vice was her deep thirst for knowledge, which was strictly forbidden to MerWomen.

Marianna finished smoothing away the tangles and ran her soft fingers lightly through Serena's hair. "There you go, my Princess." Then she turned to sift through Serena's wardrobe.

Serena stood up and tried to follow her father's footsteps in the sand, but her gait was much wider than the slow measured steps of a Turtle. She walked over and fell across her four-post bed made from hand-carved coral and embellished with an intricately hand-woven seaweed drape canopy. A fisherman's net filled with decorative pieces of coral and seashells hung between the four posts. A great mermaid masthead, confiscated from an old Spanish galleon, served as Serena's headboard, while a treasure chest stuffed with a pirate's booty lay at her feet.

"This is one of my favorites." Marianna pulled out a long, slightly transparent dress decorated with pearls and shells. Serena lay motionless on the bed, staring out of her bubbled prison. She watched a tiger shark glide silently by; its powerful tail propelled its sleek, smooth body through the water. She quietly breathed in and out, wishing she could die.

"Serena," Marianna walked across the room, "come now, things could be worse. After all, Jaween is the champion of the Shark Fights. Many a MerMaiden would give the fins off her tail to mate with him."

Serena looked up. "Liar."

Marianna grabbed hold of Serena's arm and tried to pull her up, but Serena yanked Marianna onto the bed and began tickling her. The two girls giggled until they lay on their backs, exhausted.

Serena's face turned serious. "What do you think he's like?"

Marianna giggled, "I hear he's very well endowed!"

Serena sat up and made a comical, panicked face. "Not too much, I hope!"

Marianna giggled into one of the seaweed cushions, then hit Serena over the head with it. "Well, I guess you'll be finding out soon enough!"

Serena stopped laughing and sat up, listening to something. "Do you hear that?"

Marianna looked at her oddly. "I don't hear anything." Serena walked over to the bubble dome wall.

"Why it sounds like...there it is again." Serena placed her hand against the bubble wall and gazed out at the magical world. The vast ocean floor was littered with patches of huge barrel sponges and brain, elk horn and finger coral clusters. A brightly colored clown fish darted around the tentacles of a bright bed of sea anemones as they danced in the underwater currents. An octopus jettisoned by while a large stingray passed over the bubbled dome and two dolphins played tag with one another.

"I still don't hear a thing. Now come on, Serena! Let's try something new with your hair."

"There it is again!" Serena listened intensely.

Marianna was already arranging Serena's hair ornaments in front of the dresser. She held up a couple of gold-dusted seashells and a jewel-encrusted comb for Serena's inspection when she noticed Serena's seaweed dress on the floor. Marianna cried out in panic, "Serena, what are you doing?"

Serena clapped her legs together, joining the tiny suckers that lined the inside of her thighs. She lunged through the bubble wall. A jelly-like substance extended from her legs and feet, forming a long, golden, translucent tail, much like the tail of a goldfish. It felt wonderful to be in her element. Serena beat her great tail against the water and swam over the top of the domed city, just as the tiger shark had done earlier.

Each bubble was a living, breathing, cellular membrane created by the Ancient Ones as a safe haven away from the ever-encroaching Lander World. This Bubble World permitted the MerPeople to breathe air without ever having to surface. The unique properties of the bubble provided a high level of humidity, which was essential for the survival of these amphibious creatures. It also encased them with a mucoid film that helped rejuvenate their slimy outer covering.

Serena was amazed that she was still able to swim, since her body had changed drastically due to her long confinement. Her scales had worn away and her lower extremities looked very human except for the sheen of her skin, the tube suckers lining her thighs, and her oddly shaped feet. Her tail had an iridescent glow; her tendrils extended and her scales were resurfacing. Serena could feel herself returning to her true nature.

By the time Serena reached the great chalice-shaped latte stones that guarded the entrance to the city, she heard a shrill Dolphin squeal reverberate throughout the water. Marianna was closing in from behind, flapping her magnificent tail. It held a brilliant golden hue with speckles of green and fire-red. Long, transparent tendrils flapped in the current. She was scolding Serena, who paid her no attention. Serena was following the distant sound. She swam toward the forbidden cave opening that hid the underwater city. To Serena's surprise no one stopped them.

The MerWarriors must be away on a hunt, Serena thought as she beat her powerful tail against the current. Marianna tried desperately to catch up with Serena.

"Stop! Serena, stop!" Marianna's high-pitched squeals jarred Serena's sonar.

Serena, unlike other Dolphin girls, had watched the MerWarriors swim out on their nightly hunts and secretly longed to follow them into the dark ocean waters. Serena was different in other ways, too. She possessed mysterious powers that her father had done his best to suppress, but that she had secretly kept alive.

"With all respect, Your Highness, are you out of your Mermaid mind? It is forbidden for any MerWoman to go unescorted outside the cavern walls," Marianna squealed out in Dolphin.

"Yes, and you and I both know what the escorts do to the MerMaidens once they get them outside these walls!" Serena squealed.

"You're not going!" Marianna clicked out sharply.

"But I wasn't listening to anything but that mysterious sound that called to my soul. Poor Marianna, she was scared to death. She insisted that we ride our dolphin mounts. I hadn't seen Starfish since I was a young MerGirl. I still remember how sad I was the day my father took him away from me. 'You will be queen someday.' I remember his voice, 'I will not have you riding around the sea with the other Dolphin girls.' My body shook with excitement when I felt the playful nudge of Starfish's sleek spotted skin rub against me. I grabbed hold of his fin and Marianna followed closely behind.

We forged beyond the huge branches of seaweed and coral stems that hung from the great cave walls and threatened to entangle us as we penetrated the cave's opening. At last we emerged from the recesses of the cave and I felt awed by the vastness of Mother Ocean. It had been so long since I had been outside the cave.

I nudged Starfish upwards toward the pale blue surface waters. The rays of the sun burst upon me, awakening my spirit. As we broke through the water, I could smell the salted Lander air and feel the wind on my face. Marianna followed close behind. Fear filled her face as she urged her mount, Seabreeze, forward, trying to catch up. By now I had climbed on top of Starfish's back and was skimming over the ocean waves. I felt the breeze catch in my hair and felt more alive in that moment than I had ever felt in my entire life. I let go a wild cry of freedom and danced across the sea with poor Marianna trailing behind."

Dolphin Girl

Do you hear the sound of the sea
My playful dolphin girl?
Does the roar of the waves and the crash of the surf
Not send your heart a whirl?
Have you not longed to splash in the waves and
Play with your dolphin friends?
Do you not wish to dance 'cross the sky
Each night till the evening ends?
Do you not long to feel the wind in your hair
And taste the salt on your tongue,
As you ride astride the silver-tipped one
And inhale the sea breeze into your lungs?
Listen to me, my playful dolphin girl
As you skim 'cross the silvery sea.
Run wild, run free, my lovely dolphin girl,
And never let anyone tame thee!

CHAPTER TWO

"I sang praises to Mother Ocean as I danced upon the waves, grateful for my newfound freedom! I felt something incredible was about to happen that would change my life forever, and then I saw it. A derelict sailboat was foundering on the reef. I clung to Starfish and nudged him closer to the marooned ship."

"Stay away from that, Serena!" Marianna squealed. "There could be Landers inside!" But Serena had already spurned Starfish toward the faltering ship.

"Serena! Oh, curse the seas! This is the ultimate *Jahad*! Your father will never forgive me!"

"*Jahads, Jahads*!" Serena's tube suckers held tight to Starfish's sleek body. Something she could not explain was pushing her onward. "Name me one *Jahad* that the Shark Quam can commit!"

Serena's fierce blue eyes flashed anger. She had tasted freedom and liked it. "Anything that promotes freedom in a MerWoman is a *Jahad* in the eyes of the sacred Trinity of the blessed Shark God, the Holy Father Poseidon and his divine son Triton, and now Jaween! Oh fish heads!"

Serena peered curiously at the bobbing wreck, ignoring Marianna's pleas. She approached the sinking ship. The hull was ripped open. A broken door swung open. Serena dismounted Starfish and crawled up on the reef to get a better view of the stranded craft. Marianna clicked and squealed frantically, but it was no use. Serena flung open the cabin door and saw a Lander's body strewn across the bed. She smelled the stench of death.

"Serena, get back here right away!" Marianna squealed at the top of her lungs.

A wave came crashing down, splitting the hull in two and exposing a large bed. A second wave hit and pulled the bed to the edge of the reef where it teetered back and forth. There, lying on the bed, was a man face down on top of a beautiful woman. Her face was as pale as the moon and blood stained the sheets under her lifeless body. Serena mustered up her courage and turned the top body over. It was then that she saw his face. She could never forget that face no matter how hard she tried: the handsome, rugged face of a Lander Man. Underneath him was his woman. Serena had only seen death in the Shark fights, but she recognized it now. The woman was dead. The man was alive but delirious.

"He must have loved her dearly, I remember thinking, then I noticed the tiny baby clutched in his arms."

"Landers!" Marianna's squeals had reached hysterics. She pointed to a large approaching vessel. "Serena! You must come NOW!" Marianna squealed. She kicked Seabreeze into the deep waters below. Serena watched as Marianna disappeared into the safety of the deep.

"I knew in my heart I had to save the father and the child. I dragged the attached skiff over and gently took the tiny baby from the man's arms, then carefully laid the child inside the boat. I pulled the man's muscular body over to the skiff. His arms draped around me, and for a moment he opened his beautiful eyes. They were mysterious, tormented eyes. I'll never forget that moment as long as I live. I looked deep into them and felt a tremor inside my heart.

The man stared, as if hypnotized, back into my eyes, then he did his best to crawl into the small boat. I gathered the tiny Lander infant into my arms. He was so small and so fragile. *Poor little thing,* I thought, *you will never know what it is like to be loved by your mother.* A tear fell from my eyes as I remembered the deep pain of growing up without a mother. At that moment I did something very impulsive. I took my emerald necklace, the only thing I possessed of my mother, and placed it over the child's tiny neck. *Maybe this will ease your pain,* I thought.

Then I put the babe in his father's arms. The Lander opened his eyes once again and looked at me and smiled very vaguely. I heaved the tiny skiff off of the reef and watched it dance in the wind as Mother Ocean picked it up and hurled it toward the approaching ship.

Jaween! I remembered. If I didn't make it back for *Growgar* my father would surely have a nervous fit! I summoned Starfish and we sped toward the entrance of Mer. I would return to my confinement but with the memory of this fantastic adventure locked away forever in my heart."

CHAPTER THREE

Jaween entered the great palace hall with a fresh kill of dolphin slung over his back. He was easily ten feet tall. His pale bluish grey complexion was offset by the whiteness of his hair that fell over his broad shoulders. A breastplate encrusted with jewels stopped just short of his navel, exposing his rippling abdominals. Bangles of gold and silver ornamented his bulging biceps. His lower extremities were covered with a loincloth made of shark hide. Powerful frog-like legs covered with scales that glistened with turquoise and deep green bulged from under his attire. He opened his mouth, revealing pointy teeth stained black from octopus ink.

"King Halstaff!" Jaween beat his breastplate with his powerful fist, the traditional greeting of a Shark warrior. He threw the dolphin carcass at Halstaff's feet, splattering him with blood.

A swarm of hammerhead sharks clustered outside the dome walls, hungrily gazing inward at the dead catch lying on the palace floor. The domed hall was fifty feet in diameter with large stone columns lining the perimeter. Banners made of hand-spun seaweed adorned with seashells depicting the great battles of Poseidon and Triton, Jaween's father, hung between each column. In the center of the room lay a long, inlaid coral table. A barbeque pit was built into the table for roasting large catches. A number of delicacies were spread upon the table: shark-fin dip, octopus tentacles, squid salad, raw grouper fingers and an assortment of delicious seaweed treats. Great fluorescent plankton chandeliers hung overhead, while large metal trays of whale oil burned brightly in stands strategically positioned in front of each banner. A chorus of TurtleBoys was assembled, ready to strike up their instruments for the king and his honored guest.

"Where is your daughter, Serena?" A deep hunger showed in Jaween's eyes as he impatiently searched the bubble hall, oblivious to Halstaff's discomfort.

Halstaff wiped the blood from his face and clapped his stubby palms together. Two servants entered and carried the unfortunate creature away.

"That's quite a catch." Halstaff was still mopping his face, trying to conceal his anxiety.

"I caught that one outside the reef this morning. A bit puny, but it's fresh meat. Where is your daughter? Did she not know of my coming?"

"She will be here soon." Halstaff nervously cleared his throat, "She is making herself ready for you. She is deeply honored by your presence and she wants to make herself look appealing." Halstaff smiled.

Jaween was already making his strange gasping noises. Since Jaween's mother, Sharfina, was part Dolphin, Jaween had inherited the need to breathe air. This, combined with his Shark nature, had created a rare genetic disorder known to the MerPeople as *Auragia*. Although his Dolphin nature required air, his Shark constitution could not properly disperse the oxygen. Jaween's skin took on a bluish tint as a result of the improper oxygen distribution. An ungodly gasping sound emitted from his mouth as he struggled to take in more air.

Sweat rolled down Halstaff's old Turtle back. "How about some shark-fin dip?" Halstaff pointed to the large seashell bowl on the table. He knew all too well that Jaween's *Auragia* would be followed by his fierce temper and acts of violence. "It's delicious."

"I don't like to be kept waiting!" Jaween turned even bluer.

"Blessings be upon you this *Growgar*." Serena's sweet voice filled the bubbled hall.

Jaween turned and bowed with excitement at the sight of Serena, who stood with her hand extended toward him. He licked it as his eyes feasted on the sleek curves of Serena's shapely body. A small bit of saliva dribbled from the corners of his mouth. He raised his hand and wiped the slobber away. His anger had been replaced with another rudimentary impulse.

Halstaff mopped his sweaty brow. Serena was dressed in a tight seaweed wrap. The artistic design accentuated her hips in a very erotic manner.

"Pardon me, my mighty warrior, but I wanted to look my best for you. I hope these rags of seaweed do not offend you." Serena moved around just enough to excite Jaween almost to the point of climax.

"No." Jaween did his best to control his passions, knowing full well that if he overstepped his boundaries the entire mating ritual could be called off. Little did he know that this was precisely what Serena was hoping for.

"Please, sit down, Jaween." Serena glided her hands over the towering mass of muscles and pushed on his fierce breastplate. He fell back onto an exquisitely carved coral chair. Serena swept her long blonde hair to the side and sat down at his feet, as all Dolphin girls were required to do. She motioned for her whalebone instrument, which was brought to her by one of the TurtleBoys. She strummed the taut seaweed strings, and a beautiful sound rang forth, complemented by her delicate voice. As she sang an alluring Dolphin song, Jaween's disposition softened. Halstaff too relaxed and secretly gave thanks to the Great Turtle Mother for his daughter's skill in handling Jaween.

Serena kept singing as two other Dolphin girls joined her. Jaween had fallen into a trance. Serena had him just where she wanted him. Serena slowly stood up and began to dance to the enchanting song. Her sensual movements accentuated her voluptuous body. She knew full well what she was doing. Her erotic dance excited Jaween. If Serena could drive Jaween to excess, if his lust overcame him and he breached the etiquette of *Kauha*...Serena winked at the Dolphin girl who picked up the beat to an erotic tempo. She moved her body in time with the sensual beat of the building music. The flames of the fire pit leapt as drool dribbled down Jaween's ink-stained mouth and his face became a deeper shade of blue.

"As I danced I could not stop thinking about the Lander's

face. With each erotic gyration of my hips I thought of the Lander. As I seductively jiggled my breasts in front of Jaween, I was wishing it was the Lander who sat in front of me. I closed my eyes and pretended it was him. *Would he even remember me? I thought.*"

Jaween's mouth was wide open as he gasped for air. Two streams of black drool trickled down each corner of his mouth. Serena gyrated her gorgeous rear end in front of him. He was about to reach out and grab it when two servants entered carrying the dead dolphin. They placed the carcass over the fire pit. The music stopped as the horrified Dolphin girls let their instruments fall to the ground. Serena turned her head away from the gory sight.

"Freshly roasted dolphin, I believe it's your favorite?" Halstaff took the opportunity to interrupt before Serena had accomplished her goal.

Jaween wiped his mouth. His hunger, as well as his passion, was excited and he walked toward the dead animal. He ripped a large chunk of raw flesh from its bones.

Serena walked to the other side of the bubble and gazed out at the ocean hopeful that Marianna had safely locked away Seabreeze and Starfish.

Jaween tore off another huge chunk of dolphin meat and gobbled it down. "This is delicious, Serena. Seasoned to perfection."

"Thank you, Jaween," Serena silently laughed to herself. *What seasoning?* She had instructed her cook to sprinkle a little brown seaweed on it knowing that the Shark's rudimentary gastronomical senses would not appreciate anything more sophisticated.

Jaween licked the bones clean, not noticing Serena and Halstaff's lack of appetite. He leaned back and let out a resounding belch. Serena, knowing this was the Shark's way of thanking her, forced a slight smile of acknowledgment. Her thoughts traveled back to the Lander and his baby. *Were they safe?* she wondered.

His stomach now full, Jaween turned his attention to

Serena. He walked over to her and placed his hands on her shoulders. He turned her around to face his towering physique. Her face came to his breastplate.

Jaween stared at her shapely breasts. "Serena, what has happened to your necklace? I have never seen you without it."

Serena pulled back from her thoughts and placed her hand over her chest, feeling for the first time the loss of it. "I, I lost it."

"Where? I'll have my MerWarriors search for it!"

"I'm not sure. I...I was swimming around outside...for a little fresh seawater, when I came in, it was gone."

"My pet," Jaween kissed her on her forehead. "When we are mated I shall see to it that you never leave the safety of the bubble palace." Jaween took off his necklace, a tanned shark hide strung with several jagged shark teeth from various great white kills. He strapped it around Serena's neck like a collar.

"You may wear this until I find it." Jaween smiled. The necklace weighed down Serena's sensual body. She forced another smile. "Thank you, Jaween. All the Dolphin girls will be sea green with envy!"

Jaween kept his hands on her shoulders and looked lustfully into her eyes. "Tonight I am here to take the necessary steps to become your suitor, and then you will be my mate and I, your king!"

"Is that the plan?" Serena said flatly. She was about to say more, but Halstaff motioned to his daughter to leave.

"Oh my dear little Serena, you are still too young to understand the effect you have on MerMen, but I have wanted you for so long." Another trickle of drool fell from the corner of Jaween's mouth as his grip tightened around Serena's shoulders.

Serena looked down at Jaween's sharp nails digging into her flesh, then deeply into his black eyes. "I am flattered, but we have not even initiated the courtship ritual and already you are taking liberties."

Jaween quickly removed his hands. "Forgive me, my Princess."

"Very well. I will leave you and my father to discuss the details and retire for the evening. I am suddenly quite tired." Serena stretched and yawned, intentionally showing off her shapely bosom under the transparent seaweed garment Marianna had chosen.

Jaween was so aroused it took everything in his power to control his hot Shark blood and stop himself from feasting on her voluptuous flesh.

Serena sensually swung her sexy bottom from side to side as she left the Great Hall. Then, she seductively turned around and with a sarcastic coo and said, "May you swim with the Great Shark God tonight, Jaween."

Halstaff stammered and puffed, "Very well, shall we draw up the agreement?"

"Send the scrolls around tomorrow." Jaween felt his groin pulsating. He must find some way to satisfy his craving. "I must leave you, may you swim with the sharks." Jaween dove through the bubble wall.

He swam the dark waters like a predator searching for some way to ease his throbbing spear. He circled the palace domes, hoping to find some unsuspecting MerMaiden in whom he could plunge his dagger. Just then he caught sight of Marianna scurrying through one of the bubbled walls. She was returning from safely tucking Seabreeze and Starfish into their bubble coral. Exhausted from the long swim, she let go a sigh of relief as she passed into the palace walls and took in a deep breath of air. *Praise be to the Great Whale Mother that none of the MerWarriors noticed me!* Just then Marianna felt Jaween's huge hands grab hold of her soft breasts. He sunk his long black tongue deep into her mouth, muffling any cries of protest, as his angry trident found satisfaction in the moistness of her maiden cavity.

"That night, as I lay on my soft seaweed bed, I couldn't get the Lander's tormented face out of my mind. I didn't hear Marianna's muffled cries. I pulled out my triton shell, which I kept hidden under my bed, and silently asked the Great Whale Mother to send this Lander back to me. I put the shell to my ear and sank into my soft seaweed bed, falling asleep to the sound of Mother Ocean."

CHAPTER FOUR

Great Whale Mother: enlightened, steadfast and true,
Please tell this MerMaiden just what she must do!
Shall I go forth and form this sacred bond,
To serve both thee and the Shark God as one?
A sign, Great Mother, is what I so desperately need
Then I shall know just how to proceed.

The room was dark, revealing nothing but three shadowy figures encircling a single oil lamp that floated in the center of a tranquil bathing pool. The smell of whale oil filled the bubble chamber as the chant turned into a low humming sound that resembled a cross between a Whale Song and Dolphin chatter.

One of the figures yanked the veil off her head, exposing seductive chocolate brown eyes shrouded by long, straight black hair, which was accented by wisps of brightly colored seaweed.

"I can't breathe! Besides, everyone knows that the Great Whale Mother is a myth." Oceania waded out of the bathing pool, revealing her heavy wet breasts. "And the Whale Women are just a bunch of old sea hags!" She had dangling shell earrings and a pearl stuck in the center of her navel. Beads of water dripped from her large brown nipples and dark almond skin. Below her navel were scales that shimmered with the iridescent glow of gold, orange and fire-red. "Serena, you know what will happen if anyone catches us doing this? Stop stalling! We've got to get you ready!"

The next veil came off, exposing Marianna. She leaned close to Serena and whispered in her ear, "I believe in the Great Whale Mother." Marianna climbed out of the lagoon,

"But if we don't get you ready, your father will have one of his nervous attacks."

The sound of the water dripping from one giant clamshell into another soothed Serena's soul. The gentle cascade of water inside the bathing pool was Serena's private retreat where she renewed her spirits. A loud groan arose from under Serena's veil. Marianna reached for an oil lamp and brought it close to the bubble wall. A wave of brightness rippled from it illuminating the chamber.

Oceania picked up a beautifully ornate seaweed veil, embroidered with seashells, and waved it in the air. "Serena! Take that thing off!"

Serena pulled her veil off, revealing an unruly mass of golden locks. Her delicate features twisted in her dainty face as she stood up revealing her sensual body. Little droplets of water fell over her pear-shaped breasts and pooled in her navel. Below this area, scales formed like pubic hair that shimmered a golden sparkle. Serena pulled her legs apart and stepped onto the warm sandy bottom of the Pacific Ocean. Marianna draped an ornate seaweed robe over her.

"Come on." Marianna pulled her out of her bathing chamber and into her bedroom behind the large seaweed drape where she sat Serena down in front of her coral vanity. "It's time."

The two MerMaidens quickly slapped shark oil onto Serena's hair.

"This is repulsive!" Serena pinched her nose as the stench assaulted her nostrils. Her protests were lost as the two MerMaidens tugged on her locks, weaving them into small tightly bound braids.

"Ouch! I can't stand this!" Serena whined.

"There are many new customs of the Shark Quam that you must grow accustomed to, my Princess," Marianna whispered, with great compassion.

"I don't know about you, but I wouldn't mind a little *Wa Aloo* with Jaween!" Oceania giggled as she turned Serena's head around to face the mirror and continued braiding her hair. Serena's heart sank.

"Still your mouth, Oceania! You have no idea what Serena may have to endure!" Marianna spoke from experience, since all this time she had kept the truth hidden about Jaween's recurrent sexual assaults.

A fire raged inside Serena's stomach and spread throughout her body. "Get these disgusting things out of my hair!" Serena ripped the braids out.

Marianna gently placed her hands over Serena's cheeks. "Shush, it's alright. You don't have to wear the braids if you don't want them. After all, you will soon be Queen of MerWorld."

"Let us pray, Marianna, that the Great Whale Mother will help me." Serena squeezed Marianna's hand.

"Great Turtle Eggs! Why is your hair still unbound? Jaween is gasping for air already!" Halstaff's round belly shook, and there were bags under his eyes. "There is no time! Grab her veil. Let us pray that Jaween does not notice."

Serena looked at her father with a solemn face. She did not move. Halstaff rushed around looking for Serena's veil.

"Here, Your Majesty," Marianna held it up and bowed. She knew all too well that no one wanted to anger a member of the Shark Brotherhood, especially Jaween.

"Do you really think my mother would have wanted this for me?" Serena's eyes groped the old Turtle's face for some sign of deliverance.

"My daughter," tears formed in the old Turtle Man's eyes as he looked into the mirror at Serena's reflection. "You know what you must do."

Serena breathed a heavy sigh as Halstaff draped the seaweed veil over her head.

The stench of shark oil still lingered in her hair. Serena felt a wave of nausea rising from her stomach as Marianna and Oceania gathered up her long seaweed train.

She was feeling quite ill by the time she reached the top of the coral steps in the Great Amphitheater. She took her place beside Jaween in front of the two great coral thrones. All of the Quams had come to witness the mating ceremony. Black octopus ink bathed Jaween's lips, fresh from his last feeding. The desperate gasping noises that erupted from his mouth were growing stronger.

"Tonight you will learn how to pleasure a MerWarrior, my Princess." Jaween whispered as the priest of the Shark Brotherhood bound their wrists together with strands of seaweed.

"At last you shall learn the art of *Wa Aloo*." Ink oozed out from around Jaween's pointy teeth.

"From the master himself."

"I closed my eyes and prayed as I had never prayed before, Great Whale Mother, please, if you do exist, send me a sign, an omen...anything... At that moment screams arose from the MerPeople as they scrambled to get out of the way of the enormous beast that hurtled toward the Amphitheater. It was truly the most amazing thing. No one in all of Mer had ever seen anything like it. The people scattered like a school of fish. MerWomen grabbed their children and ran. Even the MerWarriors shook with fear. But Jaween stood tall as the strange beast hurled through the great bubble wall and plummeted directly in the center of the great Mer arena. Silence now filled the room as a circle of MerWarriors slowly approached the beast who laid lifeless on the smooth sandy bottom. The MerWarriors held out their great tridents and Jaween was the first to probe the mighty creature. The other MerWarriors followed his lead, but the animal just lay still. The hide was a strange substance no one had ever before encountered and the tapping sounds echoed throughout its hollow belly.

Finally, to the surprise of everyone, a Lander crawled out of its great spout. Jaween quickly thrust his great spear through the poor Lander's heart, abruptly ending his life. Then, to my amazement, the Great Whale Mother answered my prayers. The second Lander to emerge from the sleeping beast was my Lander. I recognized his rugged face immediately. It was burned in my memory.

I let out a loud cry from the depths of my soul. It was so strange and so powerful even Jaween contracted. I felt my body quickly descending the steps. I could scarcely breathe with all the shark oil and the veil interrupting my vision, but I knew it was him and that I had to save his life.

I raised my voice and spoke as I had never spoken before. I told Jaween and my people that this was an omen from the Shark God himself, that this Lander was the much awaited *Kilahara*. As I spoke, two other Landers climbed out from the bowels of this enormous creature. The MerPeople began to murmur among themselves and shake their heads in agreement. Jaween could see the populace was in my favor. He lowered his spear and the three Landers were spared. I silently gave thanks to Mother Ocean and the Great Whale Mother herself."

CHAPTER FIVE

Pots, the ship's cook, a handsome black man who had endured years of abuse in a white man's navy, hurled himself against the strange bubble wall.

"Cut it out, Pots! You're never going to escape that way!" Corbin steadied himself as he touched the walls of their bubble prison, "Besides, I may upchuck and then we'll all be rolling around in my vomit. Doc, what do you make of it?"

Doc, a quite studious man, was peering through his glasses at the residue left on his fingers after touching the bubble wall. "It's like no substance known to man. It appears to be a living, breathing organism. It's resilient to anything that strikes against it, yet..." Doc pointed his finger and slowly moved his hand through the wall. "A slow constant pressure penetrates the bubble like a knife through butter."

Corbin and Pots looked at Doc's arm, now outside the bubble and waving in the ocean current.

"It immediately forms some kind of air-tight seal after the object penetrates, preventing leakage."

"Amazing!" Pots pushed his arm through.

Doc withdrew his hand. "What's even more incredible is that when I pull my hand back inside, it's completely dry except for this thin mucoid membrane."

Pots pulled his hand back and shook his hand trying to get the stuff off. "Yuck! It feels like that slimy shit you find on a fish."

"That means we can get out!" Corbin prepared to push himself through the bubble wall.

"And go where?" Doc pointed toward the bubble palace several hundreds yards in the distance. "We can't possibly hold our breath long enough to reach any place with air." Doc chuckled, "It's ingenious."

Pots stared at a large wolffish flashing its fangs as it circled the bubble, his eye darting toward Pots. A school of needlefish sped past while a jellyfish billowed in the current. "I feel like I'm in a damn fish bowl!"

"Yeah but who's the fish?" Doc smiled.

Corbin was the only one to hear the strange sound. It touched something deep within him and he spun around the bubble searching for its source. Its sweet melody wafted in and out of Corbin's soul. It was then that he noticed Serena. She swam in circles around the bubble, staring at them. As she circled the bubble their eyes followed her. Her long blonde hair billowed in the ocean current. Her slender body, her soft round breasts and her long powerful tail, which shimmered gold with hints of green and red, entranced them. She was a magnificent sight.

"That's her." Corbin mumbled to himself.

Doc stared at Corbin's eyes transfixed on the siren.

"Oh Jesus, pull out the candle wax. Let's plug up his ears and tie him to the mast!" Doc shook Corbin, trying to break him free from his trance. "Come on Ulysses, get a grip." Doc was well read on mermaid lore and legend and, being a Harvard grad, had read the *Odyssey* several times over. He knew full well a siren's power to seduce men and make them forget.

"She's beautiful," Corbin's eyes followed her as he broke free from Doc's grasp.

Serena smiled and held up a seashell and a small dagger. She carefully passed the objects through the bubble wall. Doc picked up the shell and smelled it. He made a face.

"Take a whiff." Doc handed it to Corbin who nearly passed out from the smell.

Next, she took her hands and sensually rubbed her breasts,

then nodded her head and smiled. The three men opened their mouths wide and stared.

"That's it honey, come on in here and I'll rub you down!" Pots was drooling by now.

"What, what do you think she's doing, Doc?" Corbin was trying his best to forget he was a man, a man who had sworn off women.

For once Doc was speechless. She pointed to the shell and then repeated the rubbing motion. Doc clamored out of his stupor. "I think she means for us to rub this shit on ourselves."

Serena pointed to Corbin.

"No, I was wrong; I think she means for *you* to rub this shit on yourself." Doc held the revolting substance under Corbin's nose.

Corbin's face puckered. "You've got to be kidding." He pushed it away but Serena kept insisting. She rubbed her sensual body even more vigorously.

Corbin feigned a smile. "Why don't you come in here and I'll rub it all over you sweetheart." His smile broadened as he held up the shell and fantasized himself rubbing her down.

"I think this must be some kind of shark repellent." Doc was examining a tiny portion of it as he held it between his fingers. "I read a study where the naval academy found that certain underwater plants act as a deterrent to shark attacks."

Serena was still patiently rubbing her beautiful body and pointing to Corbin.

"Go on Captain, she's determined that you try it out." Pots took a whiff. "It's not so bad." He turned away and made a face.

"Son of a bitch." Corbin smiled at Serena and smeared the repulsive solution on his chest.

Serena smiled and excitedly moved her hands rapidly over her breasts.

"God!" Corbin muttered under his breath.

Serena continued coaching him until he was up to his neck,

but he just couldn't bring himself to cover his face. Finally, Corbin managed to smear it on his cheeks. He looked up for approval but Serena had vanished. In the distance, charging toward the bubble, were several of those monstrous creatures astride large tiger sharks. They began rolling the bubble away.

Corbin, Pots and Doc knocked against each other as they were transported to the large bubble-domed Amphitheater. This was the same grand arena their sub had smashed into. Their sub was gone. The lower portion of the arena dome was now filled with water, except the very top portion, which was filled with air to enable the air-breathing Quams to grab a quick breath from time to time as they needed. The arena portion of the Amphitheater now took the appearance of an underwater bullfighting ring. The citizens of Mer took their places inside the arena, floating above carved stone seats. They anchored themselves with seaweed straps.

The sacred Shark fights were a special initiation to determine if a MerBoy could pass into manhood and become part of the revered Shark Brotherhood. It was a fight to the death.

There was no greater honor than to join the Brotherhood or to die in the great white fights. The MerWarriors lined the arena, protecting the viewers from rogue sharks and sometimes creating turbulence in the waters by stirring up the sandy bottom.

Corbin's bubble was positioned so that he and his companions could see everything. He watched as the crowd bowed their heads in solemn reverence as the MerWarriors swam into the arena. Behind them swam Serena, accompanied by Marianna and Oceania. King Halstaff was the last to enter. The crowd slapped their fins against the stone steps, and the games began.

The first warrior to enter the arena was a young MerBoy. He was pale, gaunt and had scanty hair growth. A large MerWarrior, who looked excessively aggressive, swam into the arena. He raised his long trident and cut a gash in the young boy's thigh, then swam away leaving the frightened boy behind as shark bait. The young boy floated in the center of the arena alone and waited to face whatever was approaching from the depths of the dark cave. A rusty iron gate was hoisted open by two MerWarriors while the Quams quietly gazed on. Suddenly, a twelve-foot great white darted into the center of the arena. Shrill squeals arose from the Dolphin girls as they watched the ferocious shark speed toward the warrior's bloody leg. As he darted closer he rolled back his black eyes and turned onto his side. The young warrior was unprepared. The shark grazed his leg and threw the boy backwards into a spin. Before the young warrior had time to recover, the shark was making another pass. This time the MerBoy swung his sword out to meet the shark head on, but the great white's jaws clapped down hard on his arm and bit it off.

Marianna buried her head in Serena's bosom. But Serena did not flinch; she held her head high and watched the gory sight.

The arena was filled with so much blood that the boy didn't see the shark as it made its third pass and cut his body in two. The great white quickly gobbled up the lower torso, leaving what was left of the gashed MerBoy's body floating in a veil of blood.

The crowd slapped its flippers against the stone steps as the MerWarriors contained the shark. They quickly cleared the blood and hauled off the remains of the MerBoy.

Doc looked down at the seashell filled with shark repellent, then turned to Corbin.

"Maybe we should smear some more of this shit on you."

Corbin globbed the stuff on his hands and slapped it vigorously all over his body.

"You know it really doesn't smell that bad." Corbin rubbed it vigorously on both cheeks.

Doc shook his head in agreement.

"You call that a fair fight!" Pots nervously rocked the bubble.

"Hey, you're not the guy with this stinking shark *crapola* all over you!" Corbin reminded Pots.

"You think that shit is going to protect you from those teeth?" Pots blurted out, then quickly covered his mouth, realizing what he had just said.

Jaween swam toward the bubble; he stuck his head in and stared at the three Landers. Then he looked Corbin in the eye and gave him an evil smile. Corbin stared into his black Shark eyes. Jaween took a deep sniff and his smile faded. He pushed himself out of the bubble.

"I guess that's my cue." Corbin stripped off his shirt and his pants.

Pots quickly took the gooey substance and stuck it in Corbin's face. "Wait, Captain, you forgot to cover the family jewels." Pots forced a smile.

"You think this crap is going to save my willie from those teeth?" Corbin pointed at the great white still thrashing about.

"I could be wrong but when we're talking about a man's personal treasure, I say better safe than sorry. Here." Pots made a motion toward Corbin's groin. Corbin's hand shot up.

"Thanks, Pots, but I think I can take it from here." Corbin dipped his hand into the repellent and opened up his drawers, then rubbed some of the repellent on his privates.

"Don't forget to cover your ass!" Pots giggled.

Corbin sighed and obliged him. Meanwhile, Doc shoved the dagger into Corbin's other hand.

"Now play nice with the other sharks."

Corbin forced a half smile then took a deep breath, tucked the dagger between his teeth, and shoved himself outside the bubble. Jaween was waiting.

Jaween took his trident and plunged it into Corbin's right thigh, making an unnecessarily large wound, then signaled to release the great white.

A huge twenty-foot great white shark sped toward Corbin with its jaws wide open and its eyes rolled back. Corbin already felt the need to surface and fill his lungs. The powerful beast lunged and Corbin darted to the left but his enemy's open jaws just kept coming. Corbin closed his eyes, ready to become breakfast, when the powerful jaws stopped short of taking a bite out of him. Instead the huge beast circled around him.

It worked, Corbin laughed to himself and surfaced for a breath of air. The little siren had been right. She had saved his bacon a second time! Corbin grabbed for his dagger. *Maybe the dagger will work too*, he thought. The shark was making another pass, but when he got within striking distance, he suddenly stopped. The MerPeople looked at one another, perplexed by such a miracle. Corbin seized the moment and thrust the dagger into the great shark. He only managed to graze him, but the poisoned tip did the rest.

As the shark thrust itself toward Corbin, it stopped in mid motion. Its eyes peered dead ahead, in a daze. Its gills continued to breathe, but the great shark's tail stopped moving. Corbin jumped on top of the great beast and sent the small dagger plunging into its black eyes. Blood once again filled the arena. When it finally cleared, the blinded shark was swimming in circles around the arena with Corbin on his back.

"Son of a bitch, it worked!" Doc slapped Pots on the back.

The MerPeople went crazy! They flapped their fins against the stone seats. Corbin had suddenly become the MerPeople's hero.

Corbin passed by Serena on the great white. He looked at her and she smiled back. Jaween saw for the first time what love looked like in the face of his woman. That look had never been there for him but now it lit up the arena. Jealousy pulsed through Jaween's powerful body.

For the first time in MerHistory a Lander had passed the Shark Brotherhood Initiation. Needless to say, it didn't go over big with the Brotherhood.

Jaween appeared armed and ready in the center of the arena. The great white was put out of its misery and Corbin was escorted back into his bubble.

"Looks like you made an enemy." Doc pointed to Jaween as he took his own trident and cut himself across the chest. The crowd grew quiet as five twenty-foot great whites were released from their cages and sped toward Jaween. The MerWarriors kicked their webbed feet and stirred up the sandy bottom, creating a blinding disturbance. The waters were so turbulent no one could see what was happening. Fins flipped about as they witnessed the gnashing of teeth and swishing of tails. Blood filled the arena and everyone let out a few bubbles of anticipation.

The MerWarriors ceased their kicking and the waters began to calm. The bloody cloud cleared and in middle were three dead sharks floating on their sides.

The remaining two sharks were fighting each other. The larger shark attacked the smaller one, chomping a large gash out of its side. When only the largest one was left, Jaween swam underneath it and pierced its belly. But this still did not stop it, and Jaween had lost the element of surprise.

The shark circled around and clipped Jaween on his right thigh. Blood once again filled the arena. The shark made another pass to finish Jaween off. This time Jaween rammed his trident into the shark's opened mouth as he charged him straight on. The shark bit down on the trident, pulling it out of Jaween's hands. The great white thrashed about trying to loosen the trident from his mouth. Jaween seized the opportunity to swim around to the backside of the shark. He pulled out a dagger that was strapped to his ankle and slit open the belly of the beast.

Jaween quickly removed the dagger and cut out a tooth from the dying shark's mouth. He swam over to Serena and offered it to her. The entire Quam slapped its fins again with overwhelming approval.

CHAPTER SIX

"The Shark Quam had abandoned their caves and now resided in a special section of the bubble-domed city. Through their inbreeding with the Dolphin Quam a new generation of Shark Quam mutants had been born. They could breathe air, but like Jaween many of them suffered from *Auragia.* Not only had this condition given them blue skin and white hair but it also created a very negative disposition. During a fit of *Auragia* a MerWarrior would become excessively violent and ill. I say excessively because violence was the basis of the entire MerWarrior culture. The only cure was for them to plunge themselves into the ocean. This way they would leach oxygen through their retracted gills and cool their hot temperament.

As for breeding, there were no more females of pure Shark Quam lineage. The Shark Quam had developed a taste for the women of the Dolphin Quam and selected them exclusively to learn the art of *Wa Aloo* in the Sacred Temple of the Shark God. Those that had successfully become skilled in the art of pleasuring the MerWarriors and proved to be of a hearty constitution became the bearers of the sacred seeds. The Shark Quam had become proficient at manipulating bloodlines so the Dolphin girls who mated with Shark Quam bore only males. Thanks to the Great Whale Mother I was spared from serving in the temple due to my royal status.

The MerWarriors hauled the great beast that brought my Lander back to me with long ropes of braided sea whips into the old abandoned Shark caves. They had pulled it from the Amphitheater where it had fallen into these interconnected underwater caves. Inside the caves were air pockets, so the three Landers would be able to live and heal their great beast in comfort. There was even a freshwater spring nearby to provide them with water. There was also a hot spring that provided steam heat and warm bathwater. This was all thanks to an underwater volcano.

The one they called Doc was very studious. If he wasn't a Lander I would have sworn he was part of the Turtle Quam. He became good friends with Ios, the oldest and most respected member of the Turtle Quam. The other one who had skin the color of a coconut they called Pots. He learned how to fish and make food for the Landers using our sea vegetables, such as dulse, nori, wakame and sea palm fronds.

The learned man they called Doc was becoming quite fluent in Shark, Dolphin and written Turtle. Why, Ios had even taught him some of the forbidden language of the Ancients, recorded by the Turtle Quam. And my Lander was trying to learn a few of the Dolphin sounds. Shark was the easiest of the three languages. It was basically composed of six very rudimentary guttural sounds. But who wanted to speak to a Shark? Turtle was next. The spoken form again was quite simple, but written Turtle was very complex. The most difficult of the three languages to speak was Dolphin. We were a very talkative Quam and had sounds and tones for everything. The language was composed mostly of high pitched squeals, clicks and a strange sort of humming noise."

Pots sat on the beach of the Shark caves. Their submarine was docked close by. They had found enough driftwood and coral to make a gangplank that led to the deck of the ship. Pots was making a queer humming noise as he scooped out fish guts, preparing the evening meal.

"Cut that out Pots, you're giving me a headache!" Corbin yelled as he stepped off the gangplank and onto the beach.

"I'm practicing my pick up lines in Dolphin. Cap, I just said what a beautiful tail you have. Mermaid girls like that. According to Ios, the shape of a Mermaid's tail is considered a source of great pride. Isn't that so, Ios?"

Doc was seated across from Ios on the beach, playing what could only be explained as Mer Chess. Tiny carved stone figures representing the four Quams were positioned on a three-dimensional game board. Each piece had a certain move it could make. For example, the Queen of the Whale Quam could move in almost every direction, while the Shark pawn could only move backwards.

Ios nodded politely, which generally was the extent of this wise old Turtle's verbal activity.

"Of course nowadays, with the introduction of their bubble-domed environment and the excessive use of their vestigial legs, their tails have lost much of their original power, as well as their magnificence." Doc sighed and moved his Seahorse. "But that's not what you said anyway."

Pots turned to him and made a strange squeal again that caused Corbin to cover his ears. "Damn it Pots! You sound like something that needs to be put out of its misery!"

Doc clicked his tongue against the roof of his mouth. You forgot the very important...," he clicked again, "sound, that suggests something pleasing to the eye. Without it you are only saying something like wow, what a tail! MerMaidens are very sensitive about their tails, especially since each one is unique, and they don't flash them around carelessly. When you talk about a MerMaiden's tail it's kind of like...talking about... well their...well, let's just say it's like telling a Lander girl she's got a great pair of..." Doc held his hands in front of his chest.

Pots's eyes lit up. "Go on!"

"So I would rethink your entire approach."

"You know they're all woman if you can just get past the tail!" Pots tossed a couple of fish on the fire.

"Tell me, Ios, whatever happened to the Whale Quam?" Doc moved his Queen into one of Ios's traps while inquiring in perfect Turtle.

Ios had learned English, or the Lander tongue, as he referred to it, from many of the ancient texts he had read before they were all destroyed. He had even learned to speak it exceptionally well after listening to Doc's pronunciation a few times, but he preferred his native tongue of Turtle and he had the annoying habit of answering all of Doc's questions with riddles or Ancient Turtle rhymes. Doc enjoyed this because it always challenged his grasp of the Turtle language, and the scholar in him respected his wise teacher.

"Crew," Ios muttered, the Turtle equivalent of check. Doc scratched his head as he gazed at the board. "Was it some kind of epidemic?"

The Turtle Quam was a very secretive Quam. They knew many things since their members were among the oldest living citizens of Mer. But they were also famous for carrying their secrets to their graves.

"Were they driven out?" Doc's curiosity was piqued as Ios captured Doc's Whale Queen.

Ah, the Whale Woman, the Whale Women.
Where are they from? Where did they go?
If you ask, nobody knows.
All but one,
Who doesn't even know
That she knows.

The wise old Turtle mused.

Corbin had climbed back aboard the *Poseidon* and was banging away on the sub when he first noticed something slithering under the smooth surface of the lagoon water. He quietly raised his hammer, ready to strike at whatever lifted its head from the deep. Doc noticed Corbin and jumped up, grabbing a piece of firewood while Pots, too, prepared for battle. The three sailors stood poised, ready to attack, when Serena's beautiful face rose up out of the water's depths. Corbin looked at her, exhaled, and dropped his hammer on the ground. Doc dropped his log and Serena clicked and squealed something in Dolphin. Marianna and Oceania swam up behind her. Ios pushed himself back from the chessboard and stood up. He started to bow but Serena stopped him with her shrill squeals. Ios obediently turned to Corbin and translated Serena's message.

"You have been invited by the queen to attend one of our most sacred ceremonies," the old TurtleMan said in perfect

English. "All the Quams will attend and you shall represent the Lander Quam."

Corbin plowed through the water aggressively toward Serena. He was covered with grease and oil and without blinking an eye he grabbed Serena by the tail.

"You can tell your flounder-faced queen that if she doesn't free me and my men right now…"

"But sir, the queen!" Ios was again interrupted by Serena's shrill squeals. She was shocked by the impertinence of this… arrogant, ungrateful Lander whose life she had saved not once, but thrice!

Serena took her great tail and knocked Corbin so hard he fell under the water. Corbin surfaced, spitting water out of his mouth.

"Captain, this MerMaiden is only trying to help! Besides, nobody is holding us. We fell into *their* world and we can't get out." Doc turned to Serena and in perfect Dolphin said, "Tell your queen we would be honored."

"I remember thinking to myself, this Lander has education and manners, too bad I am in love with the other, and just to show him my power I flicked my tail and knocked him under a second time, just as he was still trying to catch his breath. Never take on a MerMaiden in her element. She's a formidable enemy."

Serena squealed to Ios then disappeared under the waves with her two handmaidens trailing behind.

Corbin stood up spitting and coughing water out of his lungs.

"Her Royal Highness will send a bubble to transport you this evening." Ios waddled into the water then disappeared.

"Fine." Corbin wiped his face, which was smeared with oil, as he trudged onto the beach. "What the hell else do we have to do?"

Pots called out after them, "Wait! You don't have to swim off now! I just threw some fresh fish on the fire." Pots turned and looked at Doc. "Did you see the size of that brunette's..." Pots made the same gesture Doc had made before but Corbin glanced over at Pots with a look that could kill, "...tail?" Pots quickly finished his sentence.

Corbin was soaked. He pulled off his shirt and wiped the grease from his muscular chest.

"It's like I always said, if you can get past the tail they're all woman!" Pots giggled. Doc laughed and Corbin shook his head as he wrung the salt water from his wet T-shirt.

CHAPTER SEVEN

Corbin had just finished the last bite of barbequed fish when the entourage of MerWarriors entered the cave. He jumped up, ready to take them on, but Doc calmed his warrior blood when he saw the bubble encasement they had carted along.

"Take it easy Corbin, they're just here to escort us to the ceremony," Doc did his best to interpret their grunts.

"Well, you can tell them I changed my mind." Corbin stared up at Bile, a ten-foot tower of muscles that stood in front of him.

"Maybe we should humor them a bit." Doc stared at Mako, the other equally imposing MerWarrior who stared down at them with his black Shark eyes. He grinned back, exposing a mouth full of sharp pointy stained teeth.

Pots swallowed hard. "I agree with Doc, besides, a little MerCulture could do us all good."

Corbin heaved a great sigh as one of the warriors shoved him into the bubble.

"The Lander had fulfilled two of the requirements of Ancient Whale Woman lore. He had arrived inside the belly of a great beast and he had passed the Shark Brotherhood Initiation. This made Corbin a very likely candidate for the position of *Kilahara*. But what happened that evening I will never forget. It undeniably confirmed his position as the *One* in the eyes of all of the MerPeople.

Like your fable of Cinderella, the Lander and his friends were transported to the great palace in the bubble coach drawn by MerWarriors astride their Tiger shark mounts. Unlike Cinderella, they collided recklessly one against the other."

"Get your smelly feet out of my face, sailor, or that's the last time you use them!" Corbin grumbled as Pots scrambled to move off his captain and accidentally kneed him in his crotch.

Corbin's face was crushed against the bubble wall and he was crying out in pain when he noticed the pathway to the palace was lined with hordes of MerPeople bowing in homage as his bubble chariot passed by. Corbin struggled to sit up and look slightly respectable as they passed through the great stone latte Gates of Mer, a moment that had been prophesized for eons in Ancient Whale Woman Lore. In the distance were the glistening domes of the City of Mer.

Doc turned to Corbin. "Toto, we're not in Kansas anymore."

Corbin smiled and pointed. "Don't look now but there's the Emerald City."

For this auspicious occasion the three Quams had gathered from the far reaches of the Ocean Empire. The bubble was pushed against one of the large bubble chambers of the palace and the three Landers penetrated the wall and walked into the Great Amphitheater.

Doc went first, he took a deep breath, and Corbin followed. When they reached the other side their skin had a soft slimy sheen.

"Yuck! Get this crap off of me!" Pots rubbed his skin and the three Quams fell silent as everyone stared at the strangers.

"It's just a protective outer mucus coating." Doc explained.

"Well, I don't want any damn mucus on me!" Pots's face screwed up as he rubbed his hands over his body in disgust.

"Let's try and show a bit of dignity here." Corbin looked around as the MerPeople stared at them as if they were wild animals.

A tone sounded indicating it was time for the festivities to begin. The MerPeople filled the Great Amphitheater. They wore finely woven clothing adorned with precious jewels and shells. The women had their hair swept up into elaborate hairdos accentuated with sparkling jewels, seashells and strategically arranged clumps of colored seaweed. The men wore robes of finely spun seaweed. Their scales glistened in the soft fluorescent plankton glow. Soft music played in the background.

Suddenly a band of MerWarriors marched into the amphitheater. They plodded in two by two with Jaween in the lead. There was a quiet murmur, and the MerPeople bowed as Jaween passed by. He was extravagantly decorated with a jeweled breastplate, gold bangles, and an elaborate fuchsia-colored seaweed robe that trailed behind him. His huge muscles gleamed with the slimy mucoid coating.

"Now, that mucus crap looks good on him," Pots whispered.

Jaween turned, "It's the *Kilahara!*" Jaween laughed and his MerWarriors joined in with their powerful voices.

Jaween grunted something in Shark to Bile who grabbed Corbin and Doc by the arms and led them to their seats.

Corbin, Doc and Pots were seated in a place of honor beside the two empty thrones. Music played and King Halstaff entered with a beautiful MerWoman beside him. She was breathtaking. She had long tan legs and blonde hair done up in an elegant hairdo. Her face sparkled and an elaborate dyed seaweed garment adorned with brilliant jewels and precious shells accentuated her sexy figure. Corbin gazed into her beautiful face.

"Doc, there's something very familiar about that MerWoman," Corbin whispered in Doc's ear as the MerWarriors left them and marched to the center of the arena. Corbin's eyes remained transfixed as the MerWoman looked down upon him and gave him a regal smile.

"Good Lord, It can't be..." Corbin's mouth was wide open.

Doc smirked. "Our little MerMaiden cleans up pretty nicely."

"But Doc, she's got legs!" Corbin tried to hold back his enthusiasm. "Mmm, this presents all kinds of possibilities."

"Look around the room Captain, everyone has legs."

Serena was more beautiful than any woman Corbin had ever seen. She held herself erect and proud and looked like a true queen, not the playful Mermaid splashing around the lagoon. He couldn't keep his eyes off of her. Serena's eyes caught Corbin's and there was a smirk on her lips.

"Looks like Serena has taken you for a ride, Cap," Pots snickered.

"That little siren!" Mischief flashed in Corbin's eyes. "We'll see who takes who for a ride!" Corbin smirked back with a determined gleam.

"The sound of drums pierced the silence. The MerWarriors, those distinguished members of the Shark Quam who had passed their initiation and survived the Shark fights, had the honor of being first in all ceremonies. A chorus of MerWarriors beat the war drums. These were made from sharkskin hides spread tightly across turtle shells. A separate group grunted Shark chants in rhythm with the beat of the drums. A warrior donning the hide of a great white shark with open jaws entered the arena and began dancing to the beat. All you could see was the tanned hide of the shark draped over the towering frame and the huge gaping mouth filled with white teeth. The face of the MerWarrior was hidden so it looked as if the shark was really alive. The rhythm of the drums intensified, and so did the chanting. The shark dancer's movements also heightened in time with the tempo. The audience, led by the Shark Quam, began to grunt in Shark. My heart beat in time with the rhythm of the drums. Until finally, the dance and the chanting reached a climax.

The dancer collapsed in the center of the arena; his body went into convulsions. Slowly, with a great deal of groans and guttural sounds that were frankly quite unnerving, the dancer arose. At that moment the dancer had been transformed into the Shark God himself by the magic of the drums and the chanting. He danced fiercely around the room trying to frighten and intimidate the other Quam members. His body wriggled and darted about and he lunged with his great jaws at audience members, attacking in the same manner as a great white would. Squeals of fear erupted from the MerPeople. Finally, the Shark God walked up the center stairs and took his honored place beside me.

Next, the Turtle Quam orchestra entered playing a wondrous melody from instruments crafted from dried sharkskins wrapped across the turtle shells, whale bones strung with seaweed and conch shells. The melody had a soothing quality that was a welcome relief after the Shark Quam's brazen exhibition of crude force. The audience relaxed and hummed to the soft Turtle tune. Another dancer clad in a turtle shell entered the room. His motions were slow and deliberate. The dancer reached a point of transformation but in a much less dramatic way.

Finally, a chorus of Dolphin girls entered, singing a beautiful tune. It was a combination of high-pitched hums and squeals. This MerMusic was mesmerizing. A dancer clad in dolphin hide danced playfully around the room in time with the mysterious music. She jumped and leaped and moved about in the same frolicking manner a dolphin would.

At last all the Quams joined in together in the grand finale. The Shark Quam chanted as their Shark God danced and the other Quams followed. Everything flowed in perfect harmony: the music, the voices of the Quams, and the dancers who interwove their movements beautifully.

A young TurtleBoy made his way up the steep steps carrying a seaweed cushion upon which was an elaborate jewel-encrusted crown. He stopped beside my father, who picked up the crown and placed it upon my head. At that moment I was overcome with a tremendous power that burst forth from my very soul. I fell into a deep trance and opened my mouth. Out poured the most incredible sound. Like the Dolphin girls it was definitely otherworldly, but unlike them, it possessed power. A power that made the Shark God look downright silly in his blatant display of brute force. Within this power was a healing quality that seemed to lift my people's spirits, transporting them to another time, to another place, to another dimension.

Whereas before, with the Shark Quam, I had felt my heart pound, this time I felt my whole being vibrate. It was as if every cell in my body was humming, pulsating to the rhythm of this magical song that flowed through me."

Corbin looked around the room as everyone listened with their entire beings to the mystical sound. Their spirits were being catapulted along with the music to another dimension. It was then that Corbin noticed a swift movement out of the corner of his eye.

The so-called Shark God had grabbed Serena and was covering her mouth. Corbin instinctively pulled Serena from the Shark God's grip. With one great shove he managed to knock the massive creature off balance. The creature tumbled backwards, rolling down the steps of the Great Amphitheater and landing in a heap in the middle of the arena. His formidable shark costume had been knocked off, exposing the head of Jaween.

The MerPeople were abruptly jerked from their exalted state. They stared down at the fallen Shark God. Jaween jumped to his feet and picked up the costume sprawled out beside him.

"You! You Lander! You dare to defile the Shark God." He grunted and looked at the crowd, "Blasphemers! You will all pay dearly for this!" Jaween jumped through the bubble wall and swam away.

The Quams began to whisper among themselves. Slowly they all began to chant the same words. The chant grew in force until the entire bubble was vibrating with the words, *"Kilahara, Kilahara, Kilahara!"*

Serena smiled down at her people and looked over at Corbin.

"Ironically Jaween's actions had sealed my Lander's destiny. He was now without any doubt the undisputed *Kilahara*. The prophecy had been made manifest. The Lander had defeated the Great Shark God and awakened the spirit of the Great Whale Mother within their queen. Once again hope rose in the hearts of the citizens of Mer."

Corbin lay awake trying to get his mind off of Serena. It was true that as a man he felt aroused by the mystery of her, but there was something more, something in her eyes that stirred a deeper emotion, an emotion he had wanted so hard to never feel again.

She wasn't like Rachel—sure, she was half fish—but it was more than that. Serena was defiant. Rachel, to her own detriment, had always let Corbin lead the way, even when she sensed he was making a mistake; she still let him make it. Serena, like him, was a natural-born leader. She had spunk. He had never encountered a woman like that before. To make matters worse, he couldn't help but think of the passion he felt for her. It was a dangerous combination. A powerful ruler and a beautiful siren whose sight alone could make a man lose his senses. Corbin felt like a fish on a hook and the truth was, while part of him was falling in love, the other part of him hated himself for it.

CHAPTER EIGHT

The three stranded sailors worked feverishly to finish the aft of the sub. Pots and Doc smelted what little metal they could salvage while Corbin stood chest deep in water hammering metal sheets over the great hole. Corbin wiped the sweat from his face and was about to take another swing when Serena's face emerged out of the water beside him.

Corbin hit his thumb. "Goddamn it! I wish to God you would stop doing that!" Corbin sucked his sore thumb.

Serena stood up. Her long golden hair draped strategically over her exquisitely naked body. Corbin swallowed hard as Doc and Pots turned around. Pots stumbled over the fire and burnt himself. He let out a loud yelp, but for once Doc didn't bother to turn around.

"I came to thank you for last night." Serena spoke slowly and deliberately. She was careful to pronounce the Lander words correctly.

"You speak Lander!" Corbin smiled.

"I was instructed by Ios." Serena lowered her head modestly then looked curiously at their encampment. "How are your accommodations?"

Corbin tried not to stare at her sexy body. Even though her long blonde hair covered the more obvious areas it seemed to make her even more alluring.

"Well, your...Lander is much better than my Dolphin." Corbin swallowed and felt himself growing hard.

"Do you have sufficient food to feed your big fish?" Serena reached out her hand toward the submarine as if she wanted to pet it.

"Big fish?...uh, as well as can be expected...considering." Corbin headed her off, trying his best to control his natural urges. He licked his lips and wrung the handle of his hammer. "Would you like to see my big fish...I mean the sub?"

"Big fish?" Doc's sarcastic tone caused Corbin to wince. Corbin glanced over his shoulder at Doc. He knew Doc was reading his mind.

"You are working very hard." Serena noticed the sweat dripping down Corbin's chest. "You must be hopeful to return to your home world?" Serena searched Corbin's eyes.

"Uh, yes." Corbin knew he didn't sound convincing. The truth was, he only wanted one thing at the moment.

"I sure can't wait!" Pots joined Doc who was ankle deep in the water.

Corbin stepped in front of Pots's view. "Pots, don't you have something to do?"

"No Captain, I dun finished everything!"

"And this is the learned man and healer?" Serena walked toward Doc.

She gracefully separated her legs and stepped out of the water onto the sandy beach. When she reached the shore she had shed her mucoid encasement; the remnants lay like a jellyfish in the sand around her feet. Like Aphrodite rising from the half shell, and the men all stared at this beautiful creature emerging from the blue lagoon. Corbin had the rear view and couldn't keep his eyes off her aft.

"Ios has told me a great many things about you." Serena studied Doc's face while he blushed, doing his best not to glare at Serena's nudity.

Corbin interceded. "Come on, Your Majesty, I'll show you the repairs we have made on our..." Corbin cleared his throat and moved between Doc and Serena, directing her attention to the submarine, "big fish."

Serena turned her gaze toward the sub. "Yes, I would love to see your big fish."

Doc quickly took off his shirt to offer it to her. "Your Highness, aren't you forgetting something?"

Corbin gave Doc a dirty look.

"Oh yes." Serena reached out and took the shirt. "Sacred vestments." She slowly looked at the clothing the three men were wearing. Serena put one of her arms awkwardly into the sleeve, briefly exposing her rosy nipple in the struggle.

"Here Your Majesty, let me help." Corbin held out his hands, torn between helping her put the shirt on and cupping her sweet breast with his hand. *They looked so tender and ripe. Just the right size,* Corbin thought.

Doc's sober hand reached out and effectively held the arm so Serena could put the shirt on. Like a protective father figure about to hand his daughter over to a wolf, he pulled the shirt together and buttoned it up snugly, all the way to the top.

"All right!" Corbin pushed Doc away. "You made your point!" Corbin pulled Serena by the arm.

"Does your Lander God require all Landers to wear sacred vestments?" Serena asked Corbin as he pulled her toward the sub.

"Well, not necessarily..." Corbin was interrupted by Doc.

"Now, Captain, you know our Lander God requires sacred vestments at all times when we are above the water. He is very strict about that and it is dangerous to offend him," Doc shouted.

"I think that's enough out of you Doctor." Corbin led Serena toward the hatch. "Go smelt some more metal!"

"We don't have any more metal, Cap!" Pots shouted.

"Then...stand guard!" Corbin slid down the ladder and waited for Serena, when he couldn't help but notice the view. Although Doc had taken great precautions in covering Serena's bow there had been no provisions made for her aft, and it was now plainly visible in all its glory. Corbin struggled, trying to raise enough gentlemanly discipline to pull his eyes away. But instead he simply froze, gazing up at the magnificent sight.

Serena suddenly lost her footing and fell on top of Corbin in a rather precarious position. He wasn't sure whether he wanted to get up or not.

This, however, did not faze Serena who was too fascinated by her new surroundings. Excited by the thrill of everything, she jumped up clicking and squealing with excitement.

Corbin was still flat on his back in the middle of the floor when he realized Serena was curiously running her hands over everything she saw. He rushed to halt Serena's mischief.

"Please! These are very delicate instruments." Corbin pulled her close. "Don't you want to sit down and talk?"

Serena slipped out of his grip and ran into another compartment. "Everyone thinks this is a Great Whale that you Landers made sick so she spat you out."

Corbin slipped around and cut her off.

"You fooled them all!" Serena stared into Corbin's brown eyes and giggled. Corbin hung his muscular arms from one of the many pipes running across the top of the *Poseidon* and leaned into Serena, taking advantage of the close quarters.

"Well, we didn't exactly try to." Corbin's sailor blood was hot as he made his move on the Mermaid Queen.

"What are these?" Serena coyly slipped under his arm and ran over to the sonar, playfully moving the knobs around.

"Hey! Stop that!" Corbin tried to contain her but it was like trying to stop an octopus. Serena was now fondling the radar equipment.

"What's this?" Serena squealed with delight.

Corbin grabbed the headsets from her roving hands and put them back into their place.

"This is how we know where we are going. We listen to the sounds as they bounce off the ocean floor."

"Like the whales." Serena smiled.

Corbin looked into Serena's brilliant blue eyes and sighed.

He leaned in to kiss her but Serena was gone. Corbin sighed again. "How about a drink? I sure could use one."

"A...drink?" Serena's expression was blank.

Corbin pulled Serena into the tiny galley. He ripped through the drawers looking for one of Doc's many hidden bottles of gin. *There's the ticket!* He found another of the last bottles Doc had stowed away. He pulled down two cups and poured straight gin into them. *This will help take the edge off.* He poured a little extra into Serena's and handed it to her. "Here's looking at you, kid." Corbin looked down at Serena's nipples poking through Doc's shirt, "And what a look it is." He knocked back his gin.

Serena watched him curiously, and did the same. Corbin stared at the beauty, but she didn't flinch.

"How about another?" Corbin smiled.

Serena's eyes looked like those of a two-year-old. "Okay."

Corbin pulled out the bottle he had tucked safely away. "There's nothing that a little gin can't cure, I always say." He poured her another stiff one and they both knocked them back.

Serena was feeling a growing warmth in her chest. She unbuttoned a couple of the top buttons on her sacred vestments as Corbin licked his lips.

"How about one more." Corbin was feeling quite happy now. He poured the rest of the bottle into their cups and they both downed the gin.

Serena heaved a sigh. Her face was flushed and she ran her hand over her chest. "Oh, that's, that's very good, what did you call it again?"

But Corbin didn't have a chance to answer. Serena was already groping her next toy.

"What's this?" Serena ran her finger over a phonograph that sat on the table. She picked up a forty-five rpm record that lay beside it.

"This?" Corbin took it from her childish hands. "It's a phonograph, here, I'll play it for you."

Corbin put the record on and the musty clarinet tune rang out *Strangers on the Shore,* filling the bowels of the metal beast. It was slow and romantic.

Serena's eyelids drooped. She was so beautiful. She smelled of the sea but in a sweet gentle way. Her hair was drying and forming tiny ringlets around her face. Doc's shirt was now unbuttoned to her chest revealing her ample cleavage. Corbin was mesmerized.

"Whale Song!" Serena was almost in tears. "Is this the song of your Quam?"

"Well...uh...yeah...you could say that." Corbin thought about it. "One of them anyway."

"Could you show me the dance of your Lander Quam?"

Corbin was embarrassed by the request. He paused for a moment, then decided to seize the opportunity.

"Well," Corbin smiled, "we Landers...we dance...together, as couples." He gently took Serena's hand, then carefully placed his other hand inside the bulky shirt through a button hole Doc had forgotten to close. He cleared his throat as he moved closer and spoke softly into her ear.

"Just follow my movements, like this." Corbin exhaled a hot breath into Serena's ear that sent chills down her spine that made her nipples stand on end. He felt her nipples harden through the shirt and smiled as he realized he hadn't lost his touch.

Serena pulled back. She wasn't sure if she liked these Lander movements, but Corbin whispered again in her ear, "Just relax, I've got you." The softness of his voice, along with the strength of his body, blended with the melody of the clarinet and of course the gin coursing through her veins, caused Serena to let go. She flowed with the moment like she did with the currents of the ocean.

Since the ear thing was working, Corbin gently put his mouth toward Serena's ear and hummed the familiar tune.

It had precisely the effect he wanted. Her body softened and surrendered into his. He was in control; he had quieted her fears. Serena let the song flow through her as she melded into Corbin. Their two bodies rhythmically moved in perfect synchronicity with the music. It was the most erotic, most sensual moment Corbin had ever known. Never before had he felt a woman so in tune with him, with the music, with the moment.

She was reaching out with more than just her body: she was caressing him with all of her soul. A wave of panic gripped Corbin's stomach. He wanted to pull back but he couldn't stop any more than Serena could. *I have seduced hundreds of women but they never had this effect on me, not even Rachel,* Corbin thought.

He felt his arms gliding over Serena's soft sensual body. She relaxed even more as if feeling waves rolling over her. The music hypnotized her. It was the most beautiful sound Serena had ever heard and her body was now caught up in the vibration.

Who was the seducer and who was being seduced? Corbin thought as his humming turned into a tickle as his tongue gently titillated her earlobe. Corbin wanted to stop himself but he too found his body beyond all control. Serena exhaled the last bit of resistance. Her nipples were hard and she felt Corbin's fingers inching their way toward them. She wanted to pull back, but the roughness of his fingertips titillating her nipples made her melt. She looked at him and opened her mouth to protest but he gently silenced her with his hot hungry mouth. She was unprepared for such...passion, such desire. Corbin held her head back and thrust his tongue into her open mouth, muffling any protests she may have had as he reached his other hand around, cupping her bosom. They continued to sway to the music. Years of life as a sailor had taught Corbin the necessity of seducing women quickly and quietly to make his nights in port memorable ones. A flash of guilt passed through him. Was he taking advantage? He didn't even know their mating customs. To hell with it, the seduction was complete, he could control himself no longer!

Skillfully he pulled Serena further back by her hair and plunged his tongue into her moist mouth, deeper and deeper.

The warmth of his tongue in her mouth was beyond anything she had ever experienced before. She knew she should stop but instead her body relaxed even more giving herself over to him completely. Corbin greedily moved his kisses down her neck as he skillfully unbuttoned the remainder of the shirt Doc had so painstakingly secured. He pulled back the sacred vestment revealing Serena's firm round breast and rosy nipple. He plunged his hot hungry moist mouth over it. The needle scratched against the forty-five rpm record as the song ended.

Corbin peeled away the rest of Doc's shirt and grabbed hold of both Serena's breasts as his tongue ravished them. He was just beginning to loosen his trousers when Serena opened her eyes and looked at him.

"The Lander God." Fear flashed in Serena's eyes. "Won't he be offended?"

Corbin chuckled and unbuckled his belt. "Don't worry about the Lander God." He spoke softly, titillating her ear with his tongue and driving her mad. "I'll take care of him." Corbin laid Serena back against a torpedo as he prepared to launch his own inside her.

At that precise moment Doc slid down the ladder and gave an embarrassed cough as he diverted his gaze from Corbin leaning over Serena's naked body.

"Am I interrupting something?" Doc feigned ignorance.

Corbin jerked around and buckled his belt back up. "Not a Goddamn thing!"

"We've got company, it's the ex-Shark God himself and he doesn't look very happy."

"Jaween?" Fear flashed through Serena's face.

"That's right, honey." Doc smiled.

"He will kill you if he finds me here!" Serena pulled her sacred vestments around her.

"Thanks for the heads up." Doc headed up the ladder. "I'll keep 'em busy until you can..." Doc cleared his throat. "Get up here."

Corbin looked at Serena. "Who is this guy to you anyway?"

"I was supposed to mate him on the day you arrived, but you came and saved me." Serena smiled and flung her arms around Corbin's neck.

"Great! No wonder I'm not winning any popularity contests with him." Corbin gently took Serena's arms from around his neck. "Okay, okay you stay here. I'll think of something." Corbin shimmied up the ladder.

"Corbin," Serena's cry stopped him half way up the ladder. "The only reason he has allowed you to live is because he thinks you may be the *Kilahara*. You must show no fear!"

Corbin swallowed hard. "Thanks." Then he climbed up the ladder muttering to himself, "I'll be sure to remember that. Damn if only he could have come a few minutes later I would have died a happy man."

Jaween had climbed on top of the submarine while Pots and Doc watched from the beach. Mako and Bile stood beside them. Doc, fascinated by their unique anatomy, could not help staring at their strange bodies. They had bare chests and wore draped loincloths and bangles around their biceps.

Jaween grunted as he carefully walked on top of the submarine. He stopped in the middle and jumped up and down, expecting it to roll over and devour him any minute.

Corbin climbed out of the center and Jaween jumped back, holding his trident up in defense. He was confused and upset. His mouth was opening and closing, straining to get air.

"I am not afraid of your beast!" Jaween shook his trident in the air and looked at Corbin as he walked toward him on top of the sub.

"I AM NOT AFRAID OF YOU OR YOUR BEAST!" Jaween grunted loudly. "I am Jaween, Chief MerWarrior and head priest of the Shark Brotherhood, son of Triton, son of the Great Poseidon himself!"

"Sure you are," Corbin said, reassuring him.

In an angry fit Jaween threw his trident at the deck of the submarine. It broke in two.

"Oh, you broke your little forkie." Corbin looked down at the bent trident, then walked past Jaween and down the gangplank. He looked at Doc and rolled his eyes. "I think it's past somebody's nap time."

"Where is Serena?" Jaween screamed.

Corbin feigned ignorance. "Who?"

"Don't lie to me Lander! One of my MerMen saw her come in here!" Jaween pounded his fist in rage against the conning tower, leaving a dent in the side.

Corbin made a face. "Now that must hurt."

Jaween, outraged, scrambled toward the gangplank awkwardly trying to follow Corbin. Just then Serena surfaced from the belly of the beast.

"Be careful Jaween!" Serena giggled. "It may eat you!"

Jaween turned and looked at Serena as she dove from the opposite side of the sub and disappeared into the waters below. Jaween jumped from the plank into the water. He emerged in front of the bow. On the bow was the face of a shark with giant teeth. It stared down at Jaween as he swam past.

"Your beast does not frighten Jaween!" Jaween rammed his fist into the painted teeth.

Doc looked at Corbin. "Oh, now *that* has to hurt."

"You got to hand it to him, he is persistent," Doc agreed. "Hey, where's our siren queen?"

"Apparently not where I left her."

"I guess you're not going to get to finish what you started... What was that you started?"

Jaween was still ramming his fist into the sub's bow.

"Apparently not and it's none of your damn business anyway. The next time I'd appreciate you laying off the sacred vestments bit. Remember, you're a doctor, not a priest."

Corbin shouted to Jaween, "Had enough, big guy?"

Doc stared sideways at the bow. "Hey, I think he put a few dents in her."

Exhausted, Jaween walked up onto the beach. His body was cut and bruised.

"Well, you showed 'em big guy!" Corbin chastised the brute.

Pots and Doc tried not to laugh. Jaween was furious. He walked over to Corbin and looked down at him.

"How long, Lander?" Jaween cried out. "How long until YOU," Jaween panted and pointed at him angrily, "leave in that fish!"

Corbin rubbed his head and attempted to speak, "I don't know Jaween, I kind of like it here."

Jaween walked toward him ready to rip him apart.

"Okay, Okay!" Corbin held up his hands. "Well, if you can stop adding new dents to my ship and we can find some more metal..."

Pots couldn't keep his eyes off of Mako's necklace. It was strung with several large shark teeth and in the center was a large gold doubloon. Jaween noticed Pots's attraction and walked over to Pots.

"You love this, Lander?" Jaween grunted at Pots.

Pots smiled sheepishly, cowering in front of the mass of muscles.

Jaween ripped the necklace from Mako's neck and shoved it in front of Pots's face. "Is this what you have come here for?"

Pots eyes grew bigger and he shook his head.

Jaween wrapped the necklace around Pots's neck and began choking him with it. Doc and Corbin sprang forward but were held back by the two goons.

"Jaween!" Serena's sharp Dolphin squeals stopped Jaween.

He turned around in obedience, then laughed. "They are weak!" Jaween let go of Pots and he dropped to the ground.

Corbin met Jaween's stare. There was a twinge of fear in Jaween's eyes. Corbin braced for impact but Jaween walked past him toward the water.

"Come along brothers, I grow weary of playing with these weak Landers."

"Don't look him in the eyes!" Mako grunted as they passed by Corbin. The three MerWarriors dove into the water and disappeared.

Doc ran to Pots's side. "Are you all right?"

Pots had bruises on his neck and his lip was bleeding.

"Captain, it seems like they were afraid of you!" Pots winced as Doc examined his mouth.

Serena walked toward them. "They would not dare harm the *Kilahara*."

"*Kilahara?*" Doc asked.

"The Chosen One." Serena smiled admiring Corbin.

Corbin was excited by the look in Serena's eyes. He wanted to take her down below and finish what they had started but Pots was badly hurt.

Serena opened her hand, placing it over Pots's throat, and let out a Whale Song. Pots's cuts closed up and the bleeding stopped. His pain was gone.

Doc watched in amazement. The man of science was totally baffled, "How in the hell did you do that?"

But Serena only smiled gently at Pots.

"I don't know. It's something I've always been able to do, ever since I was a little girl."

Serena took off Doc's sacred vestment and handed it to him with great piety while the three men stared in shock at her voluptuous breasts. "I did not honor your Lander God. I shall try harder to obey him next time."

Then Serena turned and walked into the water waving her beautiful rear end for the whole world to see. Her legs joined together and she dove into the lagoon. Corbin wanted to grab her up in his arms and carry her back into the sub but she had vanished back into the ocean from whence she came.

"Looks like you're going to have to take care of your own big fish, Captain!" Doc whispered as he walked past Corbin.

"Damn!" Corbin watched the waters, hoping she would surface.

"She's a slippery little thing." Pots laughed.

CHAPTER NINE

For the first time in Serena's life she was scared—not just frightened, but terrified! She was terrified of the way she had felt in the Lander's arms, the way her body had responded to his touch, the way her nipples had hardened under his fingertips and her mouth had opened, welcoming the thrusts of his wet tongue. *Oh Great Whale Mother, what other thrusts would I have so gladly welcomed if we had not been stopped.* Serena sighed as she rolled over, gazing out at the peaceful aquatic world. A playful bottle-nosed dolphin swam by accompanied by her mate. The two peered into Serena's chamber as if inviting her to come and play. Could she find the same kind of happiness with Corbin? She watched as the fluorescent lamps of the palace were extinguished one by one, and smiled to herself. *At least the two dolphins were of the same species. But, the Great Whale Mother had kept her promise. She had delivered the Lander to me and stopped the mating ceremony. But was it only a temporary postponement? Jaween would not be put off forever. At least now I know there truly is a Great Whale Mother and that she and Mother Ocean are working with me.*

"The thought comforted me. Since the death of my mother I had felt so terribly alone. It had been my undying faith that had kept me connected to the Great Whale Mother and kept my mystical talents alive. With Corbin's arrival I felt something awakening deep within me, something that had been asleep for a long, long time. I was changing with each passing moment. I closed my eyes and drifted off to sleep with the taste of Corbin on my lips. But suddenly I was awakened by a strong hand clamped across my mouth. I struggled but the hold was too tight."

"I should make you pay by performing the rites of *Wa Aloo* now! A drink from my mighty spear will remind you of your place." Serena bit down hard on Jaween's hand and broke free from his grip.

"How dare you invade your queen's chamber! How dare you violate the code of *Kauha*!"

"I have not been the only one to violate it. One bound by *Kauha* must travel with an escort at all times."

Jaween grabbed Serena's arms and pushed her back onto the bed. "Besides, how can you scream with your mouth full of my sacred seed?" Jaween smiled and grabbed Serena by her hair.

If you make me perform *Wa Aloo* you had better be prepared to lose your spear!" Serena stared coldly into Jaween's eyes.

Jaween felt his mighty spear wither between his loins at the prospect. He let her go and stood up. "Very well, but when we are mated you will perform the ancient rite nightly with great pleasure." Jaween smiled exposing his sharp teeth.

"*If* we are mated, that remains yet to be seen." Serena sat up regally in her bed as if it were a throne.

"I'm warning you, Serena, don't spoil yourself with this Lander or I'll..." Jaween was gasping for air.

"Or you'll what?" Serena stood up and met his Shark eyes with her own. "You're afraid, I can smell it. You think my people may be right...you think he is the *Kilahara*!"

Jaween grabbed Serena by the throat. Anger welled in his eyes. Serena could feel his grip tightening around her neck. She could not breathe. Jaween's face turned a deeper shade of blue and he lost all reason. He was angry enough to squeeze the life from her!

"I swear by Poseidon I will kill him if you ever..." Jaween tore himself from Serena and plunged through the bubble into the salty cool waters.

"I was both frightened and furious. I tore the covers from my bed and threw a golden chalice against the bubble wall. *If only I were a MerWarrior, I would challenge him to a battle in the great arena and feed his bloody carcass to the sharks!* I felt for the first time my blood boil and a strange gasping sensation deep in my throat. I did not know what had come over me, but like Jaween, I felt the need to plunge myself into the cool waters of Mother Ocean to silence my rage. I floated in the night waters, feeling a strange urge to hunt. As a young girl I had felt these urges. Now I would act on them. I sped silently through the waters like a predator. For once I would see where my instincts led me. Jaween would not control my destiny! I was now master of my own fate. Corbin had brought back my faith and with it, my power, a power that had lain dormant but was now awakened!"

It was growing late and the Shark patrol would be coming out soon. Serena cloaked herself in darkness and silently swam toward the great cave opening. No one was around; the MerWarriors had not left yet. Perhaps they were waiting for Jaween. Soon they would be along, she must hurry. Serena swam quietly through the great opening. *If Jaween caught me this time he would certainly drag me to the Great Temple of Poseidon and force me to perform* Wa Aloo *before his inner circle of MerWarriors, or perhaps his anger would make him do something even more vile!* She had heard stories. The thought turned Serena's stomach, she swam faster through the opening of the cave and hid herself in the great coral canyon. She wanted to find a spot where she could be alone, alone with Mother Ocean. Serena always seemed to think more clearly when she was in her element. She felt closer to Mother Ocean and her prayers seemed to be carried away in the currents. Serena closed her eyes and drifted, feeling the cool salt waters caressing her. She let go of her senses and allowed her body to flow with the current.

Her unrest, confusion and frustration vanished as she floated limply, surrendering her soul to Mother Ocean's embrace. As she emptied her mind, she became aware of a presence that was watching her. She slowly opened her eyes and noticed a dark figure drifting in the coral bed close to her. The figure was completely covered in a seaweed cloak. It resembled one of those phantoms the MerPeople whispered about. They were often sighted coming from the depths of the Abyss. A chill ran up her spine as she saw the figure move within a few feet of her.

"I am Serena, Queen of the Mer Nation. Make yourself known!" Serena clicked out in Dolphin.

"It is you who needs to make yourself known." The voice spoke riddles in the ancient tongue of Whale.

"Who are you?" Serena clicked out impatiently.

"Who are you?" the voice echoed in Whale with an eerie tone.

"Stop your riddles! And tell me the truth!" Serena squealed.

"So it is truth you seek. Very well, I am one who knows your mother." The distinctly female voice droned out slowly and deliberately in the elegant language of the Ancients.

Serena could barely make out the words. "You lie, my mother sleeps on the other side of the Abyss!"

"Is that what they told you child? Lies! Your mother is alive and living among the Sacred Whale Women."

"The Whale Women?" Serena clicked out in Dolphin straining to understand, "There are no more Whale Women, only a band of unholy sea hags." Serena's eyes squinted to make out the form more clearly.

"Now, you are the one who speaks lies." The manner in which the woman spoke the Ancient Whale tongue made Serena believe she was as old as the tongue itself.

"These are not lies, they are the teachings of Poseidon." *This woman didn't even know about Poseidon. Where had she been living?* Serena thought.

"But your mother was a Whale Woman, was she not, child?" The woman sounded distressed to hear Serena speak in this manner.

"My mother sleeps on the other side of the Abyss! That is all I know of her." Seasons of repressed hurt welled up inside Serena's heart.

"Child, your mind has been poisoned! Your mother is a great and holy Whale Woman who honors our Mother the Ocean. If you do not believe me, search your soul. Have you not always known yourself to be different than the others? Do you not possess gifts and abilities that may even frighten you at times?"

The words, though difficult to accept, sent a jolt of recognition through Serena's consciousness.

"Your mother requires your presence in the Abyss. Consider yourself summoned to initiate your Whale Woman Training." With that the veiled figure that had been floating only a few feet in front of Serena vanished. Only the seaweed veil remained and was quickly carried away by the ocean currents.

Serena was pale and her body trembled as she entered the palace. She did not go directly to her room but sat on the sandy ocean floor running her hands through the sand and staring out of the bubble-domed prison she had inhabited all of her life.

Could it be true? Could everything I have been told, everything I believe, be a lie? Could the religion I have been raised on all of my life be nothing more than a collection of beliefs designed to enslave me? A conspiracy to hide the truth? Could all these laws of Poseidon be for the sole purpose of keeping the MerWomen bound in servitude?

Fear raced through her body, coupled by a deep sense of grief. A loud sobbing sound sprang forth, but it did not come from Serena. Serena turned and noticed Marianna running through the long corridor.

"Marianna, what are you doing?" Serena stood up and Marianna screamed. Serena grabbed her.

"It's me, Serena." Serena shook her and Marianna stopped her shrieking and wiped away her tears.

"I…I noticed you weren't in your bed my lady. I was worried about you," Marianna lied.

Serena couldn't help notice Marianna was trembling. She grabbed Marianna. "What's happened to you?"

Jaween had developed a taste for Marianna over the seasons, and although she had done her best to avoid him, hiding inside the palace, huddling in groups of Dolphin girls, and rarely swimming in the Shark-infested waters, this evening when Serena had turned Jaween out of her bed, he had gone to Marianna's sleeping chamber to satisfy his hunger. He had been none too gentle in the taking of her. Serena sensed there was something terribly wrong; she noticed the bruise on Marianna's cheek.

Tears poured from Marianna's eyes. Serena swept her auburn hair to the side. Marianna could no longer conceal her pain. She opened her mouth to tell her queen the truth when Halstaff's voice interrupted her confession.

"Blessed be the Shark God! What is all the noise? I thought you had been abducted!" Halstaff turned to Marianna. "Leave us!"

Marianna darted away like a small fish.

"What is this about you swimming without escorts? You know it is against the laws of Poseidon!"

Serena stared deep into her father's eyes. "Father, tell me about my mother."

"Your Mother?" Halstaff answered automatically as if in a trance, "She is dead."

"Father, I saw something tonight, something not of this world."

"Serena, I told you to stay inside the bubbled domes." Halstaff started to pull a seaweed cord, "I'll summon the MerWarriors to place extra guards around the city."

"No father, it, it vanished." Serena paused.

"Vanished?" Halstaff's old eyes looked concerned. "How could it vanish?"

"The apparition told me my mother was alive and living with the Whale Women in the great Abyss. Is that true, father?"

Fear flashed in the old TurtleMan's eyes, then he recovered. "I told you a thousand times, your mother sleeps on the other side of the Abyss." Halstaff repeated the words, trying to believe them himself.

"Father, I want the truth! I have a right to know!" Serena cried out, "Have you been lying to me all these seasons?" Tears rolled down her cheeks and there was great pain in her eyes.

Halstaff embraced his daughter and stroked her hair. "My dearest daughter, everything I have done has been to protect you, please don't ask me any more questions!"

"If you don't answer me I will ask around the Quam, the old members of the Turtle Quam, Ios should know!" There was desperation in Serena's voice.

"Mother of Whales, NO! You must never speak of her again." Halstaff did not look like himself, never before had Serena seen such fear in the old man's face.

"I will tell you the truth, if you swear you will never speak of her again." Halstaff looked deeply into his daughter's penetrating blue eyes.

Serena wiped her tears away, "I swear."

"With the strange events of the past days and the coming of this Lander maybe it is the Will of Mother Ocean that you now know the truth." Halstaff drew a long hard sigh. He dropped his weary eyes.

"Your mother is not dead, although I have not seen her for many seasons. I believe she still lives among the Whale Women in the Abyss."

"Are the Whale Women unholy sea hags?" Serena pleaded with her eyes.

Halstaff reluctantly sighed, "No, we were forced to spread that falsehood by the Brotherhood of the Shark." His voice trembled. "They were at one time the most holy of women sworn to the highest servitude of Mother Ocean."

Serena stared at her father's face; he suddenly looked so old and tired. She squinted and peered deeper into his eyes. "But why did you tell me all those lies?"

" In that moment I understood the whole of it. Perhaps

it was my mother's blood that coursed through my veins and now I could see the sinister scheming of the Shark Quam. For years the Brotherhood had conspired for the mating of Jaween and me. But the Great Whale Mother had heard my prayers and sent this Lander. Perhaps he really was the *Kilahara*. I did not know if he would be the savior of my people but he had certainly been *my* savior. I stared past my father and looked at the opening to the Shark caves in the distance. *Could this Lander really be the One?* I thought. There was only one thing left for me to do."

CHAPTER TEN

Pots was up early. Although all the compartments had been flooded in the wreck, much of the food had been sealed in airtight containers or cans. Pots still considered himself the cook, so there he was, in the galley, whistling away and brewing his horrible tasting coffee. Doc wandered in, half awake.

"Can't you cook quietly," Doc groaned. They had found another one of Doc's bottles of gin last night and Doc's head still throbbed.

"What's that clump of shit?" Doc looked down at a brown clump in the bottom of the frying pan.

"Oh, that's what they call dulse." Pots looked up and smiled. "It gives it flavor! In Japan, Takimoto said..." his voice trailed off as he thought about all the men they had lost at sea. Suddenly the sub felt so empty.

Doc picked it up and stared at it. "Wonder if this stuff would ferment."

"Put that back." Pots slapped his hand with a spatula. Doc let out a yelp. Corbin walked in rubbing his head.

"What in the hell is all the noise about?"

Pots poured Corbin a cup of coffee and held it out.

Corbin gagged, "Do you want me to throw up?"

Pots shoved his way past the two men. "Fine! I'm tired of slaving over a hot stove for you ingrates!" Pots climbed up the ladder and opened the hatch. He stuck his head out then let out a loud holler, "Great God in Heaven! Hallelujah! Praise be the Lord!" Pots screamed out, "Captain, Doc! I think you'd best take a look at this!"

"My head can't take this." Doc set his coffee down and the two of them climbed up the ladder.

Corbin's head peeked out of the hatch first. "I'll be damned!" Corbin was stunned.

By the time Corbin and Doc got across the gangplank, Pots was rolling in a pile of gold coins, nearly six feet high and twice that in diameter.

Doc walked over the plank and picked up one of the pieces of gold and inspected it. "These are *pieces of eight*, they're *even more* valuable than gold. They're worth a fortune!"

"Before you get too excited," Corbin was still turning his coin over, "part of this belongs to the U.S. government."

"How do you figure that?" Pots snapped back, forgetting Corbin's rank.

"Well, there's not much this can buy down here, right?"

"That's for damn sure." Pots bit into his coin.

"So we're going to have to get back home?"

"Yeah, Yeah!" Pots agreed. "So?"

"Well, we're going to have to smelt some of this to plug up our leak." Corbin pointed to the hole in the aft he had been working on for days.

"Sink it into the ol' *Poseidon*'s aft, now that's what I call a real waste!" Doc raised his eyebrows.

Just then Serena popped her head out of the lagoon, startling the three men as they stared mesmerized by her beautiful body strutting toward them.

"The only thing that would make this moment better, even more complete, is if there were three of them," Pots chuckled as he lay back in the gold. Just then Oceania and Marianna raised their gorgeous bodies out of the lagoon. Pots jumped up out of the gold and started to wade into the water. "Thank you Jesus, thank you Lord! You must be listening to ol' Pots today!"

"Pots, get your behind back on shore!" Corbin did his best to restrain himself.

"Yes sir!" Pots stopped in his tracks and saluted him.

Serena looked at Corbin. "I must talk to you."

Corbin cleared his throat.

Serena looked around. "Not here…"

"In the big fish?" Corbin pointed toward the sub and tried not to stare at her sensual, wet, body. Pots and Doc let out a giggle but Corbin quickly silenced them with his stare.

"Oh the sacred vestments, I'm sorry." She looked at Corbin apologetically. "May I borrow yours?"

Corbin looked confused then it registered. He quickly removed his shirt. "Uh, sure." He looked at Doc with a menacing glare.

Serena put on the shirt and turned around, clicking and squealing out orders to her two MerMaidens.

Corbin felt obliged to do the same. "Men take care of our guests and I trust you will have your hands busy so you won't be interrupting your captain!"

Pots was already wading into the water, "Don't worry about a thing, sir."

"And uh, Doc, attend to these women's sacred vestments." Corbin smiled.

"Yes sir!" Doc saluted his captain in a most patriotic manner.

Corbin made sure to catch Serena this time in his arms as she made her way down the ladder. He held her there and looked into her crystal blue eyes.

"Corbin, I must go away," Serena blurted out like a child confessing a secret.

"But you just got here." As much as he tried Corbin could not keep his hands off her.

Serena squirmed out of his arms. "No, I mean for a long time."

"But why? We're just starting to get to know each other." Corbin slid his hands beneath her beautiful golden curls.

Serena's knees went weak and her body trembled, but she remembered the apparition and Jaween's threat and turned away. "I have to leave!"

Serena knew that every day Corbin lingered here his life was in danger. She looked into Corbin's eyes.

"And you must leave too. You must return to your world!"

Corbin treated her request like a child asking for candy. He pulled her hair back and nipped at her ear. The sensation sent Serena's mind spinning while her nipples hardened. She couldn't think.

"Why, don't you want me to stay?" Corbin's hands inched their way inside her shirt and his thumbs were titillating her nipples. Serena backed up and found herself lying across a torpedo...again. *There must have been torpedoes everywhere!* Corbin made his move. He leaned over and kissed her neck, sending ripples of passion throughout her body. Serena felt herself becoming moist...just about everywhere.

Corbin's tongue was running down her body. She felt it playing around her nipples. His tongue continued to explore as her voluptuous body fell back against the hard metal of the damn torpedo. She tried to free herself, but her legs just kept opening wider. She wanted to cry out for him to stop but instead she melted into the pleasure.

Soon his wet moist tongue found its way into the softness of her open legs. Corbin masterfully drove Serena mad. She squealed out in ecstasy! Corbin moved in, titillating her deeper, faster, harder until she reached an incredible climax.

Serena screamed out and grabbed hold of Corbin. She longed for him to sink his fish deep and hard within her. Corbin fumbled with his belt but felt a strange sucking sensation on the side of his face, like he was being given a hundred small hickies. Serena had become so excited when she climaxed she had squeezed her legs around Corbin's face. The tiny suckers were sticking to Corbin's skin.

With all her will power, Serena jerked herself back, causing Corbin's speckled face to turn blue. She had not only given him a rash of Merhickies but unintentionally launched an attack on his torpedo before it could fire. A shooting pain radiated throughout Corbin's groin.

"Ouch!" Corbin's voice hit soprano as he doubled over.

"Did I cause you great pain?" Serena did not know much about the anatomy of men, Mer or Lander.

"No," Corbin gasped, "I'm...I'm fine." Corbin just wanted the little siren out of his face so he could regain his manly composure. But Serena's maternal instincts kicked in. She rubbed her hands together preparing to release her healing energy. Corbin had managed to sit up and lean his head against the torpedo.

"Did I hurt your mighty spear?" Serena inched toward him with her hands extended. "Let me heal it."

"Just leave me alone!" Corbin shouted. Serena jerked back in surprise. *What have I done to merit such anger?*

"If you will not permit me to heal you then perhaps the learned man can see to your spear." Serena left to find Doc with Corbin screaming after her.

By the time Corbin pulled himself out of the sub, wincing in pain, he knew he had arrived too late. Doc and Pots were laughing on the shore.

"How's the mighty spear Cap?" Pots chuckled.

"Want me to take a look at it?" Doc snickered. Serena stood beside him with concern in her eyes.

God, I'm beginning to hate that little siren, Corbin thought as he retreated back into the sub.

Doc smiled at Marianna. "Next time you come I'll show you some of my books."

Marianna's face turned pale. "Oh no I couldn't, it is forbidden by Poseidon's law."

"You let me worry about Poseidon's law." Doc smiled as his blue eyes showed a spark of boyhood charm.

Serena let out a squeal. Oceania appeared from behind the rocks, her shirt was half off exposing one of her bare breasts. She smiled and walked toward the other two Mermaids.

Pots walked out. "Hey, my shirt...I mean my sacred vestments!" Pots ran toward Oceania who peeled off the shirt and jumped into the lagoon giggling.

Marianna turned to Doc. "Good bye and thank you." She gave Doc his shirt and followed Oceania into the water.

Serena looked at Doc. "Tell your captain that..."

Just then Corbin stood on top of the sub. He was still in pain, but worse, his ego was bruised.

"Men we have work to do! It's time to get back into the war!"

Pots and Doc raised their eyebrows and looked at one another.

"I need you to get these distractions out of here and on the double!"

Serena felt her anger growing. "Distractions! I am the queen here!"

Corbin walked down the plank, disguising a slight limp.

"I don't see any queen, all I see is a scared little girl." Corbin wasn't sure why he was so angry, maybe because for the first time in his life a woman had ignited his passion. It was all consuming and he hated her for it!

Tears burned Serena's cheeks. "How dare you speak to me that way!"

Oceania and Marianna squealed and led Serena toward the water.

"Maybe no one else can see what a great leader you could

be, if you would just stop listening to everyone else and think for yourself for once!"

Serena stopped and looked at Corbin as if for the first time. Here was a man who could see her for who she really was. He had no political agenda and Serena knew in the depths of her soul he spoke the truth. That was why it hurt so deeply.

Anger burned in her throat and she wanted to tear out his heart as he had just done to her. Instead she tore off his shirt and threw it into the water.

"Take your filthy sacred vestments!" Serena spat on them, "I hope I never see you or your Lander God again!" Serena's tears merged with the salty water of Mother Ocean as she made her descent.

Corbin felt his own heart sink as he watched the beautiful MerMaiden disappear into the depths of the water and out of his life forever.

Doc turned to Corbin. "Well, I thought that went well. What's that on your face Captain?" Doc touched Corbin's cheek. "It looks like some kind of rash."

Pots ran over and stared at it.

Corbin touched his cheek. "It's nothing. Don't you men have work to do!"

CHAPTER ELEVEN

Whose mood changes with the ebb and flow of each tide?
Who can be as gentle as seawater bathing our lips,
Or as destructive as a tidal wave slamming against an
unprotected shore?
Who plays like a dolphin where others fear to swim?
Who is always there in our hour of need?
Who carries the wisdom of the ages in her soul,
And the power to heal in her heart?
Whose capacity for love could fill the seven seas?
She is love.
Serena,
Queen of the Sea

Serena swam past the great latte stones that guarded the City of Mer. It was a bustling metropolis of underwater life with delegates from the outer Quams arriving constantly to conduct business or consult on the latest Mer policies. They came to trade commodities or catch up on the latest news. And the latest news was Corbin.

His incredible story had spread like the great red tide throughout all of the Quams in the Pacific. By now he had become a legend. The story of the Lander swallowed whole by a huge beast and emerging alive from its belly, only to pass the Shark Initiation and defeat the Shark God at the queen's coronation. It was almost too incredible for even Serena to believe as she recalled the sequence of events.

So why am I so obsessed with this wretched Lander? Serena tried hard to push Corbin from her mind as she swam through the great cave opening. She noticed the huge rocks that had fallen over the cave entrance and compared the opening to the size of Corbin's large beast. She silently smiled to herself. *Even if Corbin did get his great beast to swim again, it would take a miraculous act from Mother Ocean to move the rocks that blocked the exit.* Serena was glad. *But why? She couldn't possibly care about such a hateful Lander!*

Serena gathered her bearings and set her course for the Mariana Trench. She had only vague memories from the ancient songs and myths she had heard when she was very young. But something deep inside seemed to propel her forward in a definite direction. She cast her body into the current and let Mother Ocean carry her toward her destiny.

At last she reached the spot where the waters grew calm, yet her whole body vibrated with excitement. *This must be the place!* Serena felt it in her soul. All at once the waters began churning about her. Fear tugged at her gut. She tried to break free but she was caught in the grip of a mighty whirlpool. She cried out, but her shrieks turned to gurgles as the water closed in around her. She let go and felt herself being pulled into the depths of the ocean. As she sank deeper, she watched the ocean water turn from the familiar blue green to deeper and deeper shades of blue. The familiar fish disappeared.

She continued her journey down into the twilight zone of the Abyss. Strange new creatures replaced the familiar old ones as she descended into depths that would crush the strongest man-made ship. Serena felt a twinge of apprehension shoot through her body as she turned and watched the last bit of light dance across the familiar light blue waters. Never before had she been this deep. She wanted to stop her descent and swim back up but something inside her urged her onward. Why had her mother summoned her now for her training? It was almost completely dark. Serena could only hear the bubbles she was exhaling burst around her. She reached out and felt the jagged walls of the trench. *No, this was asking too much!* Maybe it wasn't her mother's summoning she had sensed. Maybe these Whale Women were really old sea hags, witches of the deep who had lured her to her death in the depths of the Abyss!

Serena knew she had to still her mind of its nervous

rambling. She thought of Corbin and how wonderful he had made her feel. How much she had longed to surrender herself to him body and soul, but then she remembered his last bitter words. *I'll show him, scared little girl indeed!* Serena had always been able to hold her breath for long periods of time underwater, much longer than the other Dolphin girls. Her lungs were almost empty now and she could feel the pressure outside pressing against them. She looked down and noticed a faint glow radiating from below her, then up at the pitch darkness of the ocean. The surface was gone; she could never make it up in time to breathe. She felt the cold water surround her body as she prepared her mind for her own death.

It would be painless and I will be grieved for by the entire kingdom. Strange, Serena thought as she inhaled the cold water deep into her lungs, *the one person I will miss most is that wretched Lander!* Serena thanked the Great Whale Mother for her life, and for the few wonderful moments she had spent with Corbin. She wondered if he would miss her and she lamented the fact that she would never leave this dark underworld. She would never see his handsome face again or feel his magical touch.

Why am I not dead? she thought. *In fact, I don't even feel the need for air.*

Serena's lungs were leaching the oxygen from the water molecules as she descended deeper into the trench. The walls glowed with a strange fluorescent light. She realized she was not dead, but vibrantly alive in some altered state of consciousness. She continued her descent into the Abyss.

Creepy, iridescent fish with huge teeth and no eyes silently floated by. A deep sea hatchet, closely followed by a viperfish with dagger teeth and eyes that looked like luminescent pearls, darted about as if welcoming her into its abode. Serena glanced at their light organs glowing inside their bellies. In one massive lunge they both ended up in the expandable stomach of a large swallower fish. Without warning, she felt her descent halted. It was as if she had abruptly come to the end even though the Abyss continued below her. She felt herself being pulled into a large crack in the side of the wall. At first she fought, but realizing her struggle was futile, she relaxed her body and flowed with the current. Lamps of fluorescent plankton lined the walls producing an eerie glow. Serena was washed down a long corridor. A low humming sound vibrated from within the cavern walls. It sounded like a Whale Song sung in a mournful monotone. A dim blue fluorescent light barely lit up a figure wearing a seaweed cloak that covered her entire head and body.

Serena squealed a familiar Dolphin greeting and the figure replied in Whale Song. The melody stirred something deep within Serena.

The walls were of a slanted grey rock lined with glowing plants nestled between the rocks. Serena swam behind the figure who swiftly disappeared around a corner and into another narrow corridor. She was gaining speed. Serena hurried to keep up with her but the corridor had many twists, turns and blind spots. She pressed harder but it became apparent the Whale Woman was leading Serena to a very secret place and she didn't want her to remember the way back. Serena darted around a corner and looked for the MerWoman but she was gone. For a moment she panicked until she caught sight of her cloak whipping around one of the many corridor corners.

Serena moved her fins swiftly so she could to catch up. At last she reached a huge underwater cavern that was filled with air. She lifted her head out of the water and crawled up onto a sandy beach. Around her she could hear the powerful silence of the immense space. There were boiling pools of liquid. Her ears popped from the high pressure of the steam being released all around her. The air was hot and humid and Serena felt faint. Her body was covered with tiny beads of sweat. Water dripped from stalactites into tiny pools that bubbled and oozed. Serena did her best to follow closely behind the cloaked woman but the heat was sweltering. Suddenly a giant geyser spurted up twenty feet into the air right in front of Serena. She let out a loud scream that echoed through the gigantic space and into endless chambers as she stumbled over the soupy ground. She thought she heard the Whale Woman's voice call to her but it was an echo. Serena gathered together her courage and plodded on deeper into the murky underwater world.

Her webbed feet were swollen and her joints ached but she pressed on. At last they reached an enormous gateway that towered forty feet overhead. On the top was an enormous crystal sculpture of two whales. Their heads were touching one another. Serena stared up in awe, overcome with the magnificence of the craftsmanship.

Serena paused to rest, but the Whale Woman was leagues ahead of her by now. Serena passed under the gates staring up at the great white whales. She looked above her head at the sky that was lit up by a million tiny stars made up of fluorescent crystals. A magnificent blue hue bathed everything around her. Serena could hear the sound of surf breaking on a distant shore. Although it was dark, Serena sensed the vastness of the place. The figure appeared from nowhere and motioned her to follow toward the shoreline in the distance. She walked on until she reached the sandy beach. There was a bright light that shone on it. Its sand was a brilliant pink and blue; it glistened and sparkled in the strange light. Serena lay down upon it, melting into its softness. She closed her eyes and fell into a deep sleep.

She could hear a woman's voice in her mind. It caused her to open her eyes.

"Serena, I am Chaila, your mother."

She opened her weary eyes and looked around, realizing she had been moved and was deep inside a crystal cave. It was very dark except for a few strategically placed fluorescent plants. The lights began to brighten and Serena noticed the sides of the walls were glowing. Magnificent colored crystallized stone formations, accented with deep shades of purple, cast an enchanting glow upon the cave walls.

Serena tried to open her mouth to speak, but no words came out. She was encircled by twelve cloaked figures. One of the cloaked women stepped forward and removed her veil, revealing a beautiful and sensitive face. It was a kind face with soft wisps of golden curls that fell about her deep green eyes. A bright light shone from within these loving eyes revealing a purity of soul Serena had never before seen. She searched her thoughts for some spark of recognition, but a flood of disturbing images filled her mind. She closed her eyes hoping to shut out the violent memories.

Her mother placed her soft hand on Serena's furrowed

brow and whispered, "It's all right, you are safe, now sleep, sleep."

Serena's eyelids grew heavy and she closed her eyes. She could vaguely hear the strange rasping sounds of the Whale Women's voices in her head.

Will you tell her the truth about her father, her father, her father... the words kept rolling around in Serena's mind.

No, Chaila's gentle voice silenced them. *She must first remember that she is a Whale Woman, that is task enough for her now.*

But she must know the truth! Another voice interrupted.

There is time. Chaila gazed down upon her daughter's sweet face, implanting an image into her mind.

Serena's mind drifted back in time. She was swimming through the water with her mother. *Look closely,* Serena heard her mother's voice inside her head. She stared at the wall of water that seemed to ripple. The closer she looked, the more she realized she was looking through a window: a window into another dimension, a portal into time, a parallel universe. Fascinated, she held out her hand to touch it, but her mother pulled her back.

Chaila's thoughts penetrated her mind.

One day, you too will be called to pass through the Portal of Time, but you have much to do yet.

Serena awoke with a jolt. She was alone in the cave.

CHAPTER TWELVE

Jaween was returning from a profitable hunt. He lunged through the water tightly holding onto the reigns of his tiger shark, his booty in tow. While Serena had spent her time learning how to be One with Mother Ocean, moving in harmony with the ebb and flow of her tides and discovering her own unique current in the Ocean of Life, Jaween was busy ripping through schools of fish, terrorizing pods of dolphins and plundering the intelligent octopus community.

Since ancient times, the three original Quams (Dolphin, Turtle and Whale) had fed upon sea vegetables, seaweed, plankton and kelp rich in minerals and life force. Only the nomadic Shark Quam hunted and killed. But after their rise to power, the other Quams adopted their boorish ways. Now the Quams found themselves fighting over the leftover spoils the MerWarriors brought home.

Jaween spied Ios coming out of the abandoned Shark caves. He hid himself behind a mound of rock and grabbed the old Turtle as he swam past.

"Jaween, my lord! You frightened me." Ios trembled.

Jaween grabbed the old man by his neck, "And I'll frighten you even more if you try your riddle games with me. I want answers. Now!"

Ios did all he could to nod yes. Jaween broke his powerful grip and the old TurtleMan rubbed his neck and gave thanks to the Great Turtle Mother for his life.

Jaween stared with his black Shark eyes at Ios. "Where is Serena?"

"I don't know, my Lord!" Jaween hit him and blood came out the hole in the side of his head that served as his ear.

"No one knows where she has gone. Not even the Lander!"

Jaween backed off. "I swear to you, Ios, if she is in there with him I shall make Turtle soup of you and serve you to my MerWarriors!"

"No! I swear!" Ios was holding his bloody ear and was glad that Jaween was underwater, otherwise his *Auragia* would have amplified his jealous rage.

"What are the Landers up to?" Jaween sneered.

"They are repairing their beast with the gold you sent them, my lord."

"Good, soon they will be gone." Jaween turned back to Ios. "I want you to keep an eye on them and tell me everything they say or do." Jaween grabbed Ios and shook him. "Understand?"

"Yes!" Ios sobbed.

"And if you have any word from Serena you must tell me right away! You hear me!" Jaween shook the little TurtleMan with such force his eyeballs nearly popped out.

"Yes! My lord. I swear!"

Jaween swam off to his mother's bubble to see if she had heard any news of Serena's whereabouts.

Serena was growing stronger in the Ways of the Whale each day. She had learned much and was preparing herself for her final initiation.

Each Whale Woman must find her own life current. Serena listened as Chaila's words were implanted telepathically into her mind.

But how will I know what my life current is? Serena's thoughts responded to her mother.

When you find your true life current you will flow in harmony with Mother Ocean, not in opposition, Chaila answered in her mind with her thoughts.

But how can I trust...myself? Serena was interrupted by her mother's words in her mind.

It will not always be easy but you will learn in time, now let's practice.

Chaila turned and closed her eyes. The calmness of the water dissolved into a small funnel shape that began to swell until it became a whirlpool. Chaila swam behind the reef as the funnel grew into a destructive whirlpool, which raced toward Serena. For a moment Serena felt panic. She wanted to follow her mother and take shelter behind the reef. A blur of fish scattered to avoid the powerful onslaught of water. Serena stilled her mind and focused. She summoned the power of the deep within her and drew on all of the training she had meticulously received from her mother during their time together.

She opened her mouth and a haunting Whale Song exuded from her very soul. The calm steady vibration of her voice met with the erratic power of the turbulent waters. In a few moments the treacherous waters dissolved into a flurry of bubbles. As the bubbles cleared Serena floated peacefully in the center of them. She calmly opened her eyes and smiled at her accomplishment.

A brightly colored parrotfish was the first to venture out from the reef. Then a school of angelfish darted forth into the calm waters. Chaila appeared in front of Serena and her tender eyes were filled with pride. She embraced her daughter and stroked her long hair.

"You truly have the gift of the Great Whale Mother herself." She spoke softly, with pride.

Serena had at last received enough training to embark on her Spirit Quest. This was the final and most important initiation for a Whale Woman: to make the sacred journey to the mystical sea of bubbles. Serena set out to make the arduous voyage alone, but noticed a whale shark swimming close to her. She managed to latch onto the dorsal fin of the whale shark. It was neither a hunter nor stalker but fed on plankton and krill much like the great baleens. The only shark characteristic it possessed was that it was a fish and did not breathe air, so it had to keep moving constantly to absorb oxygen from the water. Often hunted by sharks (its only natural enemies), this shy and elusive creature did nothing but circle the globe in depths of ten thousand feet or more.

Serena took this as a good omen for her final initiation into the inner circle of Whale Women. She let the Spirit of Mother Ocean guide her and the whale shark to the place where the great blue whales communed, in the Sacred City of Bubbles. She was grateful to Mother Ocean for providing her with the aid of this whale shark.

She traveled through the deep waters with her newfound friend, swimming nonstop day and night. Serena discovered she no longer needed to emerge for air, but was able to open her mouth slightly, straining the oxygen from the water the same way her whale shark companion did. As they traveled toward the Holy City of Bubbles, Serena felt herself bonding body and soul with the unique spirit of this whale...shark.

This magnificent creature had managed to extract all the positive characteristics of both species. She had the determination and unwavering drive of the shark, which propelled her constantly onward no matter what obstacles lay ahead. This, combined with the gentle and intuitive nature of the whale, made this whale shark a very unique and admirable creature of the sea.

Serena was perplexed that she had actually found good in a shark. She giggled at the prospect of finding positive qualities in Jaween. *I suppose he is a formidable warrior and even that can be a good quality.*

Jaween entered his mother's bubble chamber. Sharfina was an anxious MerWoman, a bastardized mix of Dolphin and Shark in which all the worst traits had manifested. Her playful Dolphin attributes had given way to a treacherous cunning. All that remained of her Dolphin ways was a nagging chatter punctuated by low grunts. She had surrendered all her rights as matriarch when she mated with Triton, Jaween's father, and joined the patriarchal Shark Quam. All her property and sacred ritual items had been absorbed into the Shark Quam. During the Great Upheaval she had risen to power, appointing herself Chief Priestess of the Shark Brotherhood. She was instrumental in defiling and enslaving the sanctity of the Whale Women, completely obliterating their memory from MerWorld and replacing it with the merciless reign of the Shark God.

But she eventually fell prey to her own diabolical plan. It wasn't long before the Shark Brotherhood realized she too was a MerWoman. Since all women in the eyes of the Great Shark God were treacherous sea hags, valued only for their ability to bear large pods and bring sexual pleasure, she too found herself nudged into her own powerless prison. The only power that remained was her ability to poison her son's mind. And in that she took great pride.

Jaween proudly emptied his seaweed bag. Several deep sea bass, a grouper and an ono floundered on the dry ocean floor. Jaween picked up one of the grouper still fighting for its life and ripped off its head with his sharp, pointy teeth. His mother looked down at the catch.

"Is that all you have brought to the MerWoman who bore you? A few fish? You know how I long to feed on fresh octopus and squid!" Sharfina sneered.

Jaween lifted his white beard and pulled out a baby octopus he had hidden. He held it out to her.

"Lovely." She took it in her hands and cuddled it. She leaned down and pressed her lips to its forehead in a delicate kiss, then slurped the poor little creature into her mouth, swallowing it whole.

"Tasty, but so small! Is that all you could find?" Sharfina complained as she smacked her lips and fresh octopus ink ran down the sides of her mouth.

"My dear mother, octopi are becoming very scarce," Jaween snorted as he bit the head off of yet another fish and chopped it into pieces with his mighty jaws.

"But what of Serena? I've searched the entire ocean for her! Have you spoken to Halstaff?"

Sharfina slid her hands around her son's huge muscular

arms. "You must bed this one. Your poor father would surely return from the Abyss if he knew his heirs would not bear the crown of MerWorld. Everything he did was for this end. Even his death was so your pod would sit upon the throne! Don't ever forget this, Jaween."

Jaween spun around; rage flashed in his Shark eyes. "How can I forget it, mother, when you are constantly reminding me!" He gasped for air.

"There is talk among the Dolphin women." Sharfina stroked Jaween's beard to calm him. "Serena has been called up by her mother."

Jaween pulled away and stuffed the unclaimed fish back into his bag. He would try to unload the rest for a few precious shells, perhaps even a piece of breadfruit confiscated from the surface world.

"Dolphin chatter!" Jaween scowled.

"I'm only saying time is growing short. You must secure the bloodlines before she grows too..."

Jaween interrupted, "Too what, MerWoman who bore me? I shall find out myself what has become of Serena."

Sharfina could see Jaween's temper was rising. "Never mind, my only spawn. Don't worry, I shall speak to Halstaff myself."

She stroked his long white beard. His mouth, which had been grasping for air, relaxed.

"You must not anger yourself so my son. Go now and cool your temper in the water." Sharfina watched as his face turned back to its natural shade of pale blue. The veins under his eyes relaxed and he hurled himself through the permeable bubble skin.

She let out a long sigh of relief, "He will be the death of me yet!"

Corbin was covered in sweat and grime as he hammered the gold into flat, smooth plates. His rhythmic movements were interrupted by Ios lifting his head in the lagoon. He hammered his own thumb, then noticed it was Ios and not Serena.

"Goddamn it, how many times do I have to tell you to knock!"

"Knock? A th-th-thousand p-p-pardons, I was hoping the learned man would have time for a g-g-game of MerChess?" Ios had the annoying habit of stuttering when he was nervous and lately he was always nervous.

"The learned man is busy." Corbin shouted.

Doc hollered over to Ios. "Don't mind him."

"Doesn't anyone respect my authority around here? Damn! With all these interruptions we'll never get out of this hell hole!"

Pots stood up, wiped the sweat from his brow, and whispered to Doc, "Looks like someone we know is a little sexually frustrated!"

"You said it brother." Doc turned to Ios. "Go on down and set up the board, I'll be down in a minute."

So y-y-you have n-n-not seen our q-q-queen? Ios asked.

"I don't want to hear that siren's name mentioned again!" Corbin shouted. "And if she ever shows her little Mermaid behind around here I'll cut off her tail and hoist it as colors over the *Poseidon*!"

Doc walked over to Corbin. He was carrying a rubber mat. He threw the mat down in front of him. "Do me a favor and stand on that for a minute." Corbin looked down and shrugged.

"Please?" Doc begged him.

Corbin slowly stepped on the mat still wondering what it was all about.

Doc turned and walked toward the hatch. He looked up before he disappeared down below. "Don't move!" Then he disappeared into the ship.

At that moment, Jaween and his two thugs, Mako and Bile,

quietly emerged from the depths of the lagoon. They silently climbed up the side of the *Poseidon* and on to her deck.

Pots, who was on shore, saw them first and shouted, "Look out Captain!"

Corbin looked at Jaween. He was determined to show no fear.

Jaween stood in front of Corbin. Corbin's eyes came close to his breastplate.

"So Lander, is she in there?"

"Jaween, good to see you. What's the matter, lose your woman?" Corbin stuck his hands in his pockets. "Maybe if you'd stop breathing down her neck so much she wouldn't have to run away."

Jaween reached out his clammy hand, ready to grab Corbin by the throat.

"Hey, hands off the *Kilahara*." Corbin did his best to retain a cool front.

Suddenly, Jaween let out a scream and began jumping around. Mako and Bile joined in. The three MerMen grunted and jumped frantically.

"Hey Cap, looks like the Shark Quam has invented a new dance." Pots laughed.

The three MerWarriors danced their way to the side of the ship screaming and waving their arms, and finally hurled themselves over the side into the water below.

Mako looked at Bile still shaking from the experience. "He is the *Kilahara*."

Pots shouted from the safety of the shore, "You bet he's the *Kilahara* and he's going to *Kilahara* your scaly asses if you ever come back here again."

Bile and Mako disappeared under the water. Jaween stared coldly at Corbin, let out a frustrated yell, and then disappeared behind them.

Doc opened the hatch and climbed out of the sub,

oblivious to what had just happened. He picked up the mat and looked at Corbin. "Thanks."

Corbin smiled. "By the way, what are you doing down there?"

Doc took the pipe out of his mouth, "Oh, I rigged the batteries to the hull. If those thugs show up again we'll fry their asses."

"Good idea." Corbin and Pots laughed.

CHAPTER THIRTEEN

Serena and the whale shark swam through great forests of plankton, open seas of shark-infested waters, sea meadows, and to feeding grounds off the Great Barrier Reef. They floated past vent communities where black smoker chimneys puffed plumes of hot water rich in sulfides, some reaching up to thirty-three feet high. Around them giant clams and tub worms littered the ocean floor. Giant rays, giant squids and gigantean fish with long narrow bodies and tubular binocular eyes swam around them.

After much water had passed between them, they arrived at the entrance to the Sacred City of Bubbles. Once there, the whale shark swam low, grazing on krill and other tiny organisms. Serena swam beside her to let the gentle creature rest from the additional weight. She didn't notice the great white lurking behind the coral reef. The killer beast lunged toward the whale shark, who was too sluggish to move quickly. She had been fatigued by Serena. The great white sped toward the whale shark and grazed the magnificent creature with its sharp spiky teeth. It turned to make another pass to finish off the poor beast when Serena quickly blew a spray of small bubbles into the shark's face. The shark retreated.

Serena looked over at her beloved whale shark, who was now bleeding profusely. She knew she wouldn't last long in the open seas with a wound summoning forth all her predators.

Serena formed another large bubble. This time she sang into the bubble. The bubble glowed with a green light. She held her hands out and placed the bubble over the wound. She continued to hold her hands over the wound while the blue green light radiated. The whale shark had slowed her swim down to a crawl. She could feel the energy revitalizing her. In a few moments the wound was completely gone.

Serena sensed it was time to let her dear friend go. The whale shark circled around her, then disappeared into the depths of the sea. At that moment she felt a deep sadness, as if part of her was leaving.

She turned around to see the jaws of the great white rushing toward her, his eyes rolled back. *Just like the Shark Initiation,* Serena thought. She realized then that she had to kill this great white or it would kill her. She fluttered to the side but its sharp teeth grazed her, opening a deep wound on her right shoulder. Serena flinched with pain. She somersaulted backwards as the shark swung around for another attack. This time Serena used her Whale Woman voice. The shark stopped mid stream and floated a few feet from her face, entranced by the sound. She kept singing as she stared at its hideous, scarred and battered face. Her melody was soft and soothing and she kept singing as if her life depended on it. While she sang she slowly pulled out a decorative comb buried in her hair. It had a long, sharp pointed end. She eased herself right in front of the huge beast's face. The shark must have been at least twenty-five feet long. She stared into its black soulless shark eyes. Fear took hold of Serena and her voice stuck in her throat. The shark came out of its trance and lunged forward as Serena stabbed the sharp instrument into his big round black eye. Blood filled the water as the beast thrashed about, but Serena kept driving the weapon deeper and deeper, until it hit the tiny brain inside the creature's massive body. The mad thrashing movements stopped. Serena pushed the shark away and it rolled upside down.

Serena descended into the Sacred Sea of Bubbles still shaken from the attack. This was where the ocean plates came together, and creatures from every part of the globe gathered in communion with the blue whales. She dove down into the depths of a beautiful underwater forest filled with towering trees and endless beds of multicolored seaweed. She glided past hundreds of hammerheads as she floated in the warm waters feeling the burst of bubbles erupt upon her. The bubbles contained warm gases from subterranean volcanoes.

She looked around and noticed similar eruptions coming from the cracks in the enormous plates below. All kinds of marine life gathered in these bubbles to feed. Serena was in awe of the glorious sight. She felt her body relax in the warm waters after her long and arduous journey. She floated on her back and looked up. As her mind drifted she became aware of a strong presence. She closed her eyes and let her body ease toward this presence. As she swam she put her hand out and touched the side of what felt like a living, breathing wall. It was warm and smooth. Serena turned slowly and noticed a tiny eye. She jerked back in fright, realizing she had been resting her hand on the head of an enormous blue whale, the largest she had ever seen. She swam further back to get some perspective. It was over forty feet tall and over three hundred feet long. It made Corbin's beast look like a minnow. Her first reaction was one of panic! She wanted to swim away from the enormous creature.

She focused her mind, willing herself to be still. When she did so she could sense that this magnificent and sacred creature was trying to communicate with her. She slowly approached the great whale's tiny eye, gently resting her hand over it. Never before had she seen such gentleness in such a huge creature. Serena paused and listened to the whale as it gently sang. The decibels of her whale song could easily burst a human's eardrums, outside the safe buffering of the water. Serena listened not with her ears, but with her entire being.

The vibration soothed, healed and energized her. She felt her gaping wound closing; not only was her physical wound healing, but the horror of those past memories were being soothed away by the whale song. She was transmuting both her body and her consciousness into a higher, more refined vibration. She was filled with the flood of energy transmitted from the great beast's enormous consciousness. Serena felt that if the energy went on a moment longer, she would surely die. A tremendous surge moved through her entire body, forcing every muscle to contract in a futile attempt to resist the enormity of the energy pulsating through her. Her blood vessels pounded. She felt her insides were about to burst, and they would have burst if her mother's calm and soothing voice had not appeared in her mind. *Serena, relax, let go of your control Let the energy pass through you like the current of Mother Ocean.*

She relaxed her body and the vibration from the Sacred Whale moved through her. As it did, she felt all the pain and sorrow of the past vanish. All of the hurt at her mother abandoning her and her anger at Corbin's harsh but truthful words dissolved. She felt whole. Every cell of her body vibrated at an accelerated rate. She could feel her consciousness shifting, expanding and becoming one with that of the great blue whale.

Chaila stood inside the crystal cave deep within the Abyss. She lifted her veil and turned to face the Council of Twelve. The dark figures, still cloaked, formed a circle. There were tears in Chaila's eyes. She spoke without moving her lips. *Serena's Spirit Quest has led her to Shamana!*

The twelve figures gasped, "Shamana!"

The words echoed throughout the cave.

"This surely is the prophecy!" A raspy voice rang out.

"But what of the Lander?" Another voice spoke.

"Could he be the *One?*" Yet another voice whispered.

"Then the prophecy is fulfilled!" The same raspy voice spoke again.

"Not yet." Chaila's eyes looked upward as if waiting for a sign.

Serena held on tightly to the barnacles on the back of the great blue whale. The power with which they sped through the waters was intoxicating. She felt the aquamarine waters glide over her body. This time the bonding she felt with Shamana was in a category all to itself. She had been transported to another dimension, another reality while in the presence of this amazing creature. She didn't even realize the opening to MerWorld stretched out before her. She hated to leave this Great One's presence. She had felt such love and peace in her embrace. Her own tears mixed with the waters of Mother Ocean as she bid Shamana farewell. The magnificent creature traveled on, harmonizing the waters of Mother Ocean.

Serena swam through the hidden opening to Mer. She didn't know how much water had passed since she had left but it felt like many seasons. Even though her journey had been long and dangerous, she was filled with energy and excitement. In her heart she hated to return to the oppressive teachings of Poseidon, an ideology that made her feel ashamed of being a MerWoman, and a world where physical strength, aggression and brute force were all that were valued. All she wanted now was to find Corbin and tell him how much she loved him. He was all that mattered to her.

As a Whale Woman she knew true power came from the softness within and her connectedness to Mother Ocean and all the creatures of the sea. She was becoming one with the currents of her life as the power of the ocean surged through her body and its mysteries unfolded inside her. All she had to do was listen, not only with her ears, but with her whole being, the way the whales did. She would do that now and let Mother Ocean tell her what to do.

Serena closed her eyes and floated sensually in the sea, feeling the waters of Mother Ocean surround her. She felt totally embraced and cared for. She was so self absorbed that she did not notice Jaween stalking her like prey.

Jaween watched her delicate, graceful body float in the bubbles and felt his mighty spear grow hard. The Shark in him wanted to satisfy himself right then and there. Jaween bit down hard with his sharp teeth, drawing blood from his lip trying to take hold of his animal passions. If she had been any other MerMaiden, anyone but Serena, Queen of MerWorld, he would be deep inside her by now.

"My Queen, I have been searching everywhere for you!" Jaween's Shark blood heated as he looked at Serena with lust. "The entire kingdom has been searching for you! Your father is sick with worry. Where have you been?"

Serena stopped cold and stared into Jaween's Shark eyes. She could hear his thoughts. *He is thinking about his desire to mate with me, but behind that there is a fear...What does he fear?*

Jaween smiled and wrapped her in his powerful arms. Serena felt his slimy grip around her and sensed his arousal.

His fears had vanished as he held her body close to his. She tried to free herself but Jaween's grip was too strong. She thought of using her Whale Women ways but decided not to expose herself unless she was attacked.

"I am only escorting my queen back to her kingdom." Jaween nuzzled her ear and grunted, "I missed you!"

Serena pushed his hands away from their close proximity to her breasts. She noticed in the distance a large creature moving among the shadows. It was Corbin's great beast, drawn by an army of dolphins. She smiled and a spray of bubbles escaped. "He's alive." Serena didn't realize she had squealed her thoughts out loud.

Jaween looked at Serena's excited body and pulled her tight against his throbbing member, wishing her excitement was for him instead of Corbin. He grunted in her ear, "Yes, your Lander is still alive and I advise you to do all within your power to help him leave or he will not see another season."

"That is up to the Great Whale Mother!" Serena commanded in the Whale tongue.

"So that is where you have been." Jaween smiled, exposing his stained teeth, content at discovering her secret.

He dragged her to the chamber and threw her on the bed. Marianna and Oceania were startled by their presence.

"Send for the king, I have something of value for him." Jaween grunted.

The MerMaidens ran off. A few moments later Halstaff waddled into the chamber.

"Serena, in the name of the Shark God, where have you been child?" Tears filled the old man's eyes.

"I found this precious jewel outside the city gates at early tides, when ravenous creatures feed," Jaween said as he stared at the beauty.

Serena was certain Jaween was talking about himself.

Halstaff grabbed his daughter and held her tight. He looked up nervously at Jaween.

"Once again, thank you, Jaween, for your concern." Halstaff was politely trying to dismiss the MerWarrior. He could see that Jaween was already gasping for air and his face was turning a darker shade of blue.

Serena pulled back from her father's embrace and disappeared behind a private banner into her bathroom chamber. Halstaff stared at her with fear in his old eyes.

"Forgive her, Jaween, she is still young and ignorant in the ways of Poseidon."

Jaween licked his stained lips as he watched Serena's voluptuous body silhouetted against the drapes. "Yes, young Dolphin girls are full of restless energy. She needs to mate."

"Jaween, I promise by the next mating season you will have her as your mate," Halstaff whispered in Jaween's ear.

"I would have bedded her by now if it hadn't been for that cursed Lander." Jaween wiped his mouth as his mighty chest expanded and contracted, searching for air.

"Do not anger yourself; the repairs of their floating beast are now complete. They shall be leaving soon."

Jaween nodded, his nostrils craving salty waters.

"I'll hold you to your word and will take her by the next season whether she agrees or not!" Jaween penetrated the bubble wall, glaring coldly at Halstaff as he swam away.

Halstaff lay upon Serena's large canopy bed of carved coral. He had not been well since Serena's departure. Fear had upset his already nervous system and he had not been able to keep his food down.

"Where in the name of the Great Whale Mother have you been?" Halstaff sniveled in Turtle and he shut his eyes. "I was worried sick."

"I have been with my mother." Serena stepped out from behind the privacy panel and stared into her father's beady little Turtle eyes. She fastened a pin on her robe. "She has trained me in the Ancient Ways of the Whale."

Halstaff's face was filled with horror. He quickly sat up. "You must tell no one of this, Serena!"

"Father, I can't live with these wretched Sharks." Serena looked out at the peaceful domes. "And their cursed laws!"

"Serena, that is blasphemy!" Halstaff's breath was strained. He clutched his heart. Compassion flashed in her eyes as she ran to his side. "I'm sorry father. I didn't mean to upset you." Serena stroked Halstaff face. *How could I be so insensitive to forget about my own father? He has grown so old with worry.*

"What did your mother tell you?" Halstaff asked, searching Serena's face.

"She told me how she was forced by the Shark Quam to leave and you stayed to raise me." Serena kissed her father's cheek. "Oh father, forgive me for being so angry and ungrateful. Thank you for staying and raising me. I know you must have missed her terribly."

Sweet Chaila, always thinking of others, Halstaff thought to himself as he sighed with relief.

Serena could contain herself no longer. "And what about the Lander?"

Halstaff opened his eyes. "Serena, you must forget this Lander and mate with Jaween."

Serena jumped from the bed. "How can you ask that of me? After all they have done to us, to my mother, to the Whale Women. I will hate every creature that has the blood of the Shark coursing through its veins. I will hate them until the day I die! I tell you if I could I'd take the manhood of every one of them."

"Great Whale Mother, NO!" Halstaff found his manly voice for the first time in his life. The command in it made even Serena quiet herself. "In the name of all that is left sacred, help me! Do not let the sins of her grandmother repeat themselves. I would give all the water in the ocean!" Halstaff raised his hands helplessly in the air. "Even my own life!"

Serena stared at the old Turtle who was in tears. *Where did that come from?* Serena embraced him. He was trembling. It was as if some deep hidden part of him had emerged. "Shush now, I'm sorry to have gone and upset you again, old TurtleMan. I'm afraid I'm not very good at holding my tongue." Halstaff and Serena burst into a nervous laugh.

"No, my daughter, you never have been."

"I'm sure the Great Whale Mother will show us the way," Serena looked out of the bubble as she held her father. She noticed Corbin's great beast making another pass around the city. She released her father and rushed to the bubble wall, watching the magnificent sight.

"Has he found a way out?" Serena looked nervous.

Halstaff nodded despondently. "No. He circles the cave endlessly searching for a way out."

Serena smiled. "And he will not find it! The great seaquake blocked the entrance the day the Whale Mother sent him to me."

Halstaff took his daughter's arm and pulled himself up. He looked into her eyes and with a strong steady voice said, "He will find it and be on his way, out of our world, and out of your life. It must be so, my daughter."

Serena turned away. "What are the people saying now about the *Kilahara?*"

"They bow and chant the words *Kilahara* as the great beast passes."

Serena's eyes sparkled. "And what does the Shark Brotherhood say?" Serena watched the creature make another pass.

"They claim he is an abomination, but the people do not listen."

"Good," Serena smiled and whispered under her breath, "I must leave you father. Get some rest."

"Serena! Let him go in peace!"

"Do not worry." Serena jumped through the bubble wall and into the ocean.

CHAPTER FOURTEEN

Halstaff wanted to tell his daughter the truth, but instead a bone weary tiredness overtook his feeble body. He closed his eyes and fell into a deep sleep. Soon he was awakened by a strange sound. He opened his eyes and there was a cloaked figure standing beside his bed. The figure removed the cloak, revealing Sharfina.

"I thought I told you never to come here!" Halstaff whispered.

"Don't worry old TurtleMan, no one saw me and my business is brief, but urgent!" Sharfina walked over to him and spoke in a low voice.

"My son has waited patiently for this mating. Your daughter now sits on the throne as queen. She is alive and so are you! We have kept our bargain. Now, you must keep yours!" Sharfina's black Shark eyes stared coldly at Halstaff.

Blessed Turtle eggs, what am I to do? "What about the Lander, no one can dispute the signs about his coming." Halstaff took a breath. "What if he is the One?"

"By the Shark God, he's not the One," Sharfina's loud whisper echoed evil. "Not the one you should fear. I'll tell Jaween the truth, how long do you think you will hold him and his MerWarriors back, old Turtle!"

Halstaff swallowed hard. "Yes, I will take care of things, I promise. Only you will tell him before the ritual, you must!" Halstaff lowered his head in shame.

"Leave that to me," Sharfina smiled, exposing her sharp shark teeth set close together in a Dolphin snout. It was a grotesque sight. "I'll tell him before he comes to her bed."

Oceania squealed as she waded into the Jacuzzi. Her bosoms jiggled and swelled as they floated on top of the warm volcanic water. Doc had dug a hole in the sand and maintained a perfect temperature by adding cooled water that he filtered through a series of lava stones into the hot volcanic spill off.

"Just the thing for tired, sore muscles after a rough day on the job." Doc eased into his invention, holding a concoction of specially fermented seaweed garnished with a sprig of sea lettuce. He drained his glass, then held out his hand to Marianna. "It's okay, just wade in slowly!"

Marianna had taken up residency in the Shark caves since it was the only safe haven from Jaween. At first Doc had acted like a fatherly figure, sensing she had undergone some trauma. He was genuinely impressed by her keen intellect and thirst for knowledge. He had taken her under his wing as a kind of apprentice, teaching her biology, chemistry and even a little human anatomy. There was a tenderness blooming in the festive atmosphere of the Shark caves. It seemed love was in the air.

"Woo! This is hot!" Pots moved around, then grabbed hold of Oceania. "But not as hot as me!"

Oceania, on the other hand, had come along for the sex. She had gotten a taste of what Pots could do to a MerWoman and wanted more. Since Serena's absence the two MerMaidens had been unemployed, so they conjured up some excuse about helping the Landers. King Halstaff liked the idea of helping the Landers in a speedy departure from MerWorld, so Pots and Oceania did their best to keep the two bookworms out of their books and into their five senses.

"Hey! Hey, cut out the X-rated stuff!" Doc looked at Pots and Oceania grabbing each other by just about everything that dangled.

Captain Corbin, on the other hand, had taken up celibacy and was pouring all his sexual tension into his work. He stood chest deep in water polishing the golden ass of the *Poseidon*. He had actually become quite fond of it since Serena's departure.

"I see you have healed your big fish!" Serena squealed as

she emerged so close to Corbin he nearly jumped out of his skin.

Always amazed by Serena's body, Corbin stood staring in appreciation with his mouth wide open.

Serena grabbed hold of Corbin and kissed him hard on the mouth. He felt his pent up sexual energy skyrocket as he was about to explode. He forgot all about his golden aft and flung his arms around her.

Corbin suddenly pulled back and looked at Serena, who still had her eyes closed, lost in the kiss. "Wait a minute. You think you can just leave me for...ever! Then come back and find me waiting for you! What do you take me for?" The words had barely left Corbin's mouth when he winced at the sound of them. *Oh God listen to me, I sound like some clingy lovesick woman!*

"I'm sorry, I couldn't help it. I was with my mother." Serena tried to recreate the moment.

"Excuses," Corbin responded, still hurt. He pushed her away. What was he doing! How many times had he uttered those exact same words to all the various women he'd had in every port. The shoe was on the other foot and Corbin's manly pride couldn't take it. "Don't you have somewhere else you need to be now?" Corbin waded out onto the shore.

"No." Serena followed him.

"So I see you decided to come back and grace us with your royal presence." Corbin wiped his hands off then walked to the gangplank and onto the sub. At least there he might feel more like the one in charge.

Serena's smile faded. She had forgotten how bratty he could be. "Oh stop that!"

"Is that a command Your Majesty?" Corbin bowed sarcastically and climbed down the hatch. The truth was he himself had expected his own wife and many other women to wait patiently for his return from the sea. He just hated the fact that the tides had turned and he was the one forced to do the waiting.

Serena's temper boiled. *How could she possibly care for such an arrogant, egotistical, self centered, stupid...man?"* She took a deep breath and caught her temper, remembering how much she had missed him. Serena followed Corbin into the sub. Corbin turned around, surprised he hadn't run her off. There she was, his little MerMaiden, standing there in the middle of the torpedo room, soaking wet. Her long blond locks dripping over her round voluptuous breasts. He could feel himself growing hard. He wouldn't let her seduce him. *God he sounded just like a woman!*

"Don't you want to take me for a ride in your big fish?" Serena looked around, pretending not to know the effect she was having on his glands.

"No I don't." Corbin pushed his way past her.

Serena crossed her arms across her chest. She was mad. "You can't leave the way you came in," she teased.

"So are you happy? We're trapped in this God forsaken underworld of yours!" Corbin's vow of celibacy was facing a real challenge. He clenched his teeth and turned away as Serena moved in closer with her moist lips and her perfectly pear shaped breasts. He could sense her nipples hardening and he wanted to take each one of them into his mouth slowly and suckle them.

"Are you really in such a hurry to leave?" Serena had forgotten how handsome Corbin was. She felt her body longing for his touch as she moved closer in the cramped sub.

Corbin cursed silently as he whirled around and pulled her mouth close to his. He greedily clapped his lips over hers, taking what she seemed so willing to offer. His tongue sank into the rich moistness of her mouth and he cupped her breast with his hand while his thumb circled her excited nipple.

Corbin came up for air. "So now that you've come back you want me to stay and amuse you, is that it?"

Serena felt dizzy. She looked into Corbin's eyes, unable to register anything but how much she wanted him inside her. He smiled, satisfied at his macho dominion over her. He tickled her ear with his tongue, sending goose pimples through her entire body. Serena opened her mouth to protest, but Corbin plunged his tongue in again while titillating her nipples and spreading her thighs. His attack was swift and to the target. He would show this siren queen who was in command. Serena pushed his hands reluctantly away.

"No? We'll see about that!" Corbin slid his other hand down her stomach and pressed open her legs, wide open. Serena moaned with pleasure as he gently caressed her inside. His days of waiting were over.

"Serena, enough teasing, you're going to get what you've been asking for!" Corbin's movements became rough. He held her legs apart, kissing her while massaging her deeply, violently inside. Serena bit her lip, trying to muffle her cries of ecstasy. She pawed at him trying to stop him but his movements became more and more forceful.

She thought of Jaween and what he would do to Corbin. She had to stop him…Serena came violently. She cried out and Corbin muffled her screams with his moist lips pressed hard over her.

"Serena, I want you like I've never wanted any other woman, and I've waited for you longer!"

Serena wanted Corbin deep inside her. *But what was she doing? She was signing his death decree! Her father was right, she would have to mate with Jaween and if he found out she had spoilt herself with Corbin, he would kill him!* She pushed Corbin off with her powerful legs.

"I'm sorry, I can't!" Serena shouted as she scrambled out of the belly of the great fish and into the water below.

Corbin laid on the floor, his pants halfway undone. He rubbed his hand over his face and exclaimed, "What a Woman, ok a MerWoman!"

CHAPTER FIFTEEN

"The ocean floor would shake from time to time. At first we just thought it was the Landers' movements about the ocean. But then came the terrible sickness. It spread throughout the Quams. We had never known disease before. Death to us was not a sad event. It was simply a passage of our life current into the Oneness of Mother Ocean. We would travel to the Great Abyss and pass through the Portal of Time returning from whence we came. It was a joyous occasion to return to our source. But this sickness had cut my people's time here short; many were unable to complete their true life current. And this to the MerPeople was worse than death.

The sickness quickly spread throughout the Mer population. It first started in the more distant Quams, where large schools of fish had been found floating on top of the water.

Since we had never been confronted with disease, we were ill-equipped to deal with the suffering. The sick Quam members would make their way to MerWorld in hopes of finding food, refuge and a cure. The population of my people was rapidly declining, not only due to the disease and famine, but also because many of the MerWomen were not becoming pregnant."

"You're just fine." Doc chattered in Dolphin as he pulled himself out from between the legs of a beautiful young Dolphin girl. Marianna helped the MerMaiden up as Corbin walked through the makeshift examining room in the middle of the torpedo room.

The young Dolphin girl squealed and Marianna held up the drape.

"Oops! Sorry! Excuse me!" Corbin turned his head and backed out of the tiny space.

Doc was looking at a strange growth on the neck of an older Mermaid. He clicked, comforting her as he examined the goiter.

"You need to come back tomorrow," Doc clicked out in Dolphin, then looked at Marianna to make sure she properly translated everything. He walked over to the sink, removed his gloves and washed his hands.

"Everybody decent?" Corbin called out.

"Come on in." Doc smiled as the two Mermaids squeezed past Corbin.

"Trade jobs?" Corbin smiled, his mischievous dimples bursting out as he watched the attractive young MerWoman pass by.

She giggled and whispered the word *Kilahara*.

"It's a tough job, but somebody's got to do it." Doc smiled slyly. Marianna cast a disapproving glare, collected the instruments, then left the room.

"You wanted to talk to me?" Corbin looked at his old friend.

Doc motioned Corbin into his tiny cubbyhole of an office.

"Take a seat." Doc pointed as he sat across from him.

"Gladly." Corbin sat down.

"I can't find any reason these women aren't breeding." Doc looked concerned.

"Well, that's good news!" Corbin tipped his cap over his eyes and leaned back.

"Not really." Doc pulled out one of his books and nosed through it. "This only eliminates the MerWomen."

"Well, if they're not sterile, then..." Corbin looked Doc in the eyes, "that only leaves...the MerMen."

"Since the famine the MerWarriors have spent longer

periods of time outside the protective cavern hunting for food. They've had to travel farther to find feeding grounds and stay away longer."

"So who's complaining?" Corbin hoped Serena would take advantage of Jaween's long absences.

"Stop thinking with your Johnson," Doc scowled, "this means they are being exposed to higher levels of..." Doc stopped.

Corbin looked curiously at Doc. "What are you getting at?"

"I think I've uncovered the cause of this strange sickness." Doc removed his glasses and rubbed his eyes. "I believe it's linked to the seaquakes, which are also linked to the loss of fish and other aquatic life in the area," Doc continued.

Corbin sat up. "I just assumed it was from all the increased activity in the oceans. I mean, we are, or were, at war with Japan. You know what that means: mines, torpedoes, depth charges, oil spills, all that crap has got to affect the ocean."

"I'm afraid it is much worse than that." Doc gave a sober glance Corbin's way which caused him to feel a tingle of apprehension.

"Okay, Doc, spit it out." Corbin stared into Doc's weary eyes.

Doc walked over to a bookcase that held a few tattered books. He pulled one from the shelf and opened it to a dog-eared page. The paper was marred with water stains but the words could still be deciphered. In bold letters at the top were the words: *radiation sickness.* Corbin squinted to read the water-stained words.

"So?" Corbin shrugged.

Doc began to read, "Radiation sickness causes skin abrasions, cancerous growths, thyroid disease such as goiters, usually malignant. Look at this." He held out a picture that was very hard to make out. "It looks exactly like the growths we've been seeing on the MerPeople."

Corbin squinted. "I can't see a Goddamn thing!" Corbin slammed the book shut. "Are you trying to tell me that we have been radiating the ocean?" Corbin turned away. "Why would we do a stupid thing like that?"

"I remember hearing about this fellow named Einstein working on a real hush-hush theory. I don't know, but he may have figured it out."

Doc was absorbed in his own thoughts. Corbin hated it when Doc went into one of his intellectual, self-induced monologues. He knew the guy was a genius but at least he could have the decency to clue him in on his insights in a language he could understand.

"What are you talking about, Doc?" Corbin interrupted.

"I'm talking about a bomb, a bomb bigger than anything you or I have ever seen...an atomic bomb." Doc stared coldly into Corbin's face.

"An atomic bomb?" Corbin couldn't believe the words but he'd been around the military long enough to know that inventing bigger and better ways of blowing things up was just part of the game. He had also been around Doc long enough to know that behind his sharp intellect was a keen sense of intuition. If Doc said it, you could take it to the bank.

"That's the only thing that can account for these high levels of radiation," Doc sighed.

"Wait a minute, if it's true and these scientists did learn how to build this atomic bomb..." Corbin reflected, "What kind of maniac would explode a weapon like that in our oceans?"

"Worse than sterilization and disease was the slow starvation that was now claiming over half of MerWorld's population. Out of desperation a few of my people had eaten some of the dead fish, only to die shortly after their consumption.

Since the Landers' attempts at finding an alternative exit for their submarine had failed, they decided to focus their energy on helping my people. With Jaween and the

MerWarriors away hunting for food I had plenty of time to work with Doc looking for a cure for the radiation sickness. I did my best to avoid Corbin's sexual advances but..."

Doc's weary eyes stared into a microscope.

"Doc! Doc I think I found it." Serena slid down the ladder and ran through the corridor of the sub. Corbin cut her off as she jumped through one of the hatches.

"It's customary to ask permission of the captain to board his vessel."

Serena sighed and dropped her hands, which held a glob of assorted seaweeds and a large horseshoe crab. The submarine had grown smaller by the day with Serena and Doc working side by side and Corbin's jealousy on the rise.

"Permission to board your big fish, sir." Serena smiled.

"No," Corbin stared coldly at her, "it's bad luck to have a woman aboard a submarine." His eyebrows rose. "Even one with a tail."

Serena could sense his jealousy. "Look Corbin, I'm sorry..."

Doc grabbed Serena's hand and pulled her past Corbin. "Come on, Serena, I've been waiting for you."

Serena forgot her excitement. Tears filled her eyes as she held up her find for Doc to see. Doc took the crab and the seaweed from her and placed it in a tank.

"Oh Doc, he doesn't even realize..." Serena cried.

"I know." Doc put a fatherly hand on Serena's back. "But what you are doing is right. He needs to get back to his world."

Serena swallowed her tears and dropped her head, nodding in agreement. "I thank the Great Whale Mother for sending you." Serena's gentle voice startled Doc. She gently placed her hand on his shoulder.

Doc turned around and looked at Serena's erotic body with just about everything revealed except for a few dripping tendrils that scantily covered her mounds of flesh. "Yeah, well it looks like it's sacred vestment time."

Doc gave a quick gasp and ripped off his shirt, throwing it over her. He quickly turned around and poured himself a cup of green liquid, then downed a shot of it. "And I thank the Great Whale Mother for giving me something that I could ferment." Doc smiled and winced as the liquid burned his throat. "Smooth!"

"You have done so much for my people. What more can I do to help?" Serena stepped closer. Doc took another swig and coughed.

"Well, you can start by putting on those, uh, those sacred vestments." Doc turned around. Serena put on his shirt. *God I hope Corbin doesn't walk in.*

"I could also use someone to help me run experiments and tend to the sick. Just as long as they're not more women!" Doc moaned.

"Okay, you can have Ios. He can be trusted. I'm afraid if the MerWarriors find out that Landers are behind these seaquakes you may all be in danger."

"How did you know that?" Doc turned around and looked at Serena flabbergasted.

"Whale Woman intuition."

"Well then, it will be our little secret." Doc looked into Serena's eyes.

Serena smiled. Doc looked up as Corbin walked in. He winced as he saw a jealous flash in Corbin's eyes.

"What little secret?" Corbin smiled a sarcastic smile.

CHAPTER SIXTEEN

"Between my Whale Woman knowledge of Mother Ocean's seaweeds and her aquatic life and Doc's medical skills we came up with a serum made from the blood of horseshoe crabs. It seemed to retard many of the effects of radiation. After we had treated most of those infected we decided to tackle the overwhelming problem of starvation. Most of the food outside the cave was infected, so it became apparent that we would have to return to the diet of the ancients, which was principally vegetables of the sea. We would have to grow our own within the protected cavern of MerWorld."

"With this new strain of plankton we can cultivate seaweed beds and harvest the plankton at a much greater rate. It's fortified in nutrients so it will beef up the immune system of the MerPeople, making them less susceptible to the effects of the radiation." Doc pulled back from the microscope.

"That's wonderful, when can we start seeding the beds?" Serena took a look into the microscope.

"I'll send you and Corbin out tomorrow."

"Corbin?" Serena's eyes flared.

"Pots is working with Marianna and Oceania in the infirmary; Ios and I have to create the new strain. You can't possibly plant and harvest by yourself, that leaves Corbin."

"But will he do it?"

"Leave him to me." Doc raised the test tube filled with green solution and took a swig.

The next morning Serena surfaced inside the lagoon and found Corbin sitting on the beach waiting for her.

"Hello." Serena looked surprised to see Corbin smiling and sitting on the sandy beach.

"Hi." Corbin dropped his head. "I guess I've been kind of a...jerk." Corbin looked into Serena's face. "And I'm, I'm sorry. Doc helped me to see things straight last night." Corbin looked up and Serena noticed his swollen lip.

"How are things in the city?" Corbin smiled then winced remembering his lip. He touched it in pain.

"What happened?" Serena reached for his lip but Corbin turned away.

"Oh, I...I bumped into...uh...one of the pipes."

"Oh." Serena nodded. "Worse every day. We've lost most of the old MerFolk and now the children." Tears filled Serena's eyes. "Oh Corbin, what kind of Lander could do such a horrible thing?" Corbin held her close and stroked her long, blonde hair. He took a deep sigh and looked up above.

"If only I could save the children." Serena sobbed again.

"Hey, Hey." Corbin lifted her beautiful chin. "That's no way for the Queen of MerWorld to behave."

"I don't feel like a queen, I feel like a scared child."

"You have been more of a queen since this crisis began than I ever thought possible."

Serena's sobs quieted and she lifted her head. "Really?" She looked up at Corbin sniffling, "But you said I was a spoiled brat."

"And you were, but that young girl is gone," Corbin took Serena's face in his hands, "and a strong, determined leader has emerged."

Serena smiled. Corbin moved forward to press his lips over hers but Doc's familiar voice stopped him.

"Hey, you forgot your breathing apparatus!" Doc came running toward them with a strange contraption waving about in his arms.

Corbin backed away. "Oh yeah, I forgot, I wouldn't be much good to you without that."

Doc placed the awkward contraption made from the hide of a Portuguese man-of-war over Corbin's face and inflated it with air. He looked ridiculous.

"Don't worry, you'll get used to it." Doc smiled.

"I'm not sure I want to." Corbin's voice sounded pinched and nasal.

Serena grabbed Doc's chin in her hand and turned his face toward her. Doc had a beauty of a black eye. It was swollen, purple in the center with brown and blue hues fanning out.

"Did you hit the pipes too?" She gently touched his eye.

"Pipes?" Doc looked at Corbin who was nodding his head behind Serena. "Oh yes, the pipes? Treacherous things."

"I want to thank you for knocking some sense into Corbin." Serena smiled, then disappeared into the lagoon.

Corbin ran after her with the silly device dangling from his face.

In the day of the Whale Woman the market had been a common place where precious shells, coins, jewels and occasionally contraband fruits confiscated from the surface world were traded. But with the rise of the Shark Quam all open commerce had been restricted to only the members of the Brotherhood. Now with the Shark Quam away the space was once again filled with gaiety and splendor.

It was the inauguration of the first MerMarket held during the reign of the Shark God. They had decorated the MerAmphitheater with brightly colored balloons made from blowfish, which spiraled up to the top of the bubble dome. Colored seaweed banners of deep crimson, amber and green hung from the ceiling creating a festive atmosphere. Young MerMothers had brought the few MerChildren who had survived for dolphin rides and other festive activities.

Hung high over the mercantile compartments were even a few tapestries depicting ancient Whale Lore, which the MerWomen had spun along with seaweed garments and fine jewelry. Beautifully handcrafted hair ornaments, seashell masks and pendants filled the vending stalls that formed a circle in front of the great trench. Food stands stood ready waiting to be filled with the city's first new crop of seaweed, plankton, and sea vegetables.

Serena entered the marketplace on this festive opening day with Corbin by her side, followed by Doc, Marianna, Pots and Oceania. The citizens of Mer crowded around them. They were adorned in their lavish robes of brightly colored seaweed embellished with pearls and seashells. A band of TurtleBoys beat their sharkskin drum and blew conch shells in celebration of the great opening day.

"Greetings, citizens of Mer!" Serena squealed in Dolphin, since most everyone understood spoken Dolphin. "I know we have been through some very difficult and disheartening times. We have lost many of our loved ones before their life current was complete."

The MerFolk looked around at the thin crowd. They fell silent.

"But we have not been defeated! In fact we have become stronger. And I swear to you we will not only overcome our difficulties but will flourish as we once did in the days of the Scared Whales. Today I bring to you the first harvest." Serena waved her hand and MerMen entered carrying baskets of the freshly harvested sea vegetables, plankton and assorted seaweeds. "This is only the beginning."

The MerPeople cheered.

"These Landers..." Serena motioned to the three sailors, "have found a way to return MerWorld to its ancient days of glory!"

The people cheered loudly and Serena smiled at Corbin. Then the chant rose, first quietly and then to a deafening proportion. "*Kilahara, Kilahara, Kilahara!*"

Could it be this Lander really is the Kilahara, *sent by the Great Whale Mother to help me restore MerWorld to its former glory?* Serena thought as she smiled and waved. Her eyes caught

Corbin's eyes and they both smiled tenderly at one another. *Could there be a place for our love?* Serena imagined the Statues of Poseidon crumbling and in their place the Temples to the Great Whale Mother rising as they had once stood long ago.

A gut-wrenching grunt rose from the midst of the crowd. It shattered the MerPeople's chant. "And what about your sacred vow to my son Jaween and the Shark Quam? At this very moment he hunts in strange waters with other brave MerWarriors risking their lives to bring you back the bounty you have become accustomed to."

Sharfina's fat body was helped upon the stage in the middle of the marketplace by her own personal bodyguards. She walked over to Serena and picked up one of the sea vegetables, holding it limply in her hands. "They bring you fresh squid, octopus, dolphin, grouper, snapper, and the delicacies you have grown accustomed to under the Shark Quam's rule." Sharfina smelled the seaweed. "Bottom feeders wouldn't even eat this!" She threw it at Serena's feet.

The MerPeople mumbled among themselves.

"Your...queen has forgotten her promises to her people since she passes the days with these unholy Landers."

Corbin stepped into Sharfina's fat face. "Just a minute..." Two of the MerWarriors who were standing at Sharfina's side held up their tridents.

"Sharfina," Serena bowed, "I am sure both you and I want what is best for the Quams, but whether it be the Shark or the Whale who guides us remains to be seen."

Sharfina was about to let Serena have it when Halstaff's voice interrupted. He entered the marketplace surrounded by his council of TurtleMen.

"My dear Sharfina." Halstaff waddled over. "Let me assure you my dearest daughter has not forgotten her oath to your son or the Shark Quam. In fact Serena will be setting the date for the mating ceremony when Jaween returns."

Halstaff put his claw-like hand on Serena's shoulder and

pulled her away from Corbin. Serena inhaled then let out a long sigh. She walked away with her father and Sharfina.

Sharfina stared into Serena's face. "Well, she had better hurry or she will grow too old to give my son a large pod!"

"Come, let us all enjoy the festivities," Halstaff announced, and he motioned to the TurtleBoys to strike up the band. He glared back over his shoulder at Corbin.

Serena turned to Corbin and smiled a sad smile. She watched several MerChildren holding onto the fins of dolphins outside the bubble walls, racing to see who could reach the finish line first.

"Just like the old days," an old MerWoman seated in front of a table of beautifully hand crafted seashell hair ornaments whispered. Serena broke from her father's side and rushed over to the old MerWoman.

"Do you remember the days when my grandmother ruled?" Serena's hand captured one of the coral sea fans and handed the woman some sea lettuce. This currency replaced the customary squid payment created by the Shark Quam, since squids were nowhere to be found.

"Could you tell me about my grandmother? What happened?" Serena's eyes pleaded.

"Don't ask me to speak of such things. I'm not saying what they did to your grandmother was right. It's unthinkable what they put her through, but her revenge! It was ...unholy!"

"What did she do?" Part of Serena wanted to hear the truth, and part of her didn't.

"The chain of events all started when Queen Chat'an, your grandmother..." the old MerWoman looked around, "...but it is forbidden to speak of it."

She held up a necklace. On the end was a small triton shell cut in half. "For the *Kilahara*."

Serena smiled, she opened her Mermaid's pouch made from the covers of shark eggs to give her more sea lettuce, but the old MerWoman stopped her.

"Tell him our prayers to the Great Whale Mother are with you and him," the MerWoman whispered, then backed away.

Corbin playfully flung a seaweed wrap over Serena, the shells dangled around her face. She looked exotic with the thin veil hiding part of her face.

"You are so beautiful!" Corbin stared at her mesmerized.

Serena was still unnerved by the words of the old one. *"The sins of my grandmother." Those were the words Halstaff had used. What horrible atrocity could she have done that would cause him to willingly forfeit his own life rather than have them repeated? I must ask my mother,* Serena thought.

Serena placed the shell necklace around Corbin's neck. She touched Corbin's chest where the beautiful shell fell and felt the reassuring warmth of his heart.

"It's beautiful." Serena touched the soft seaweed and looked deeply into Corbin's eyes. She wanted to kiss him but she knew it would be too great a risk. She was distracted by Pots's loud laugh.

Oceania had wrapped Pots, including his face, in several seaweed wraps, and he started moving around with jazzing, swing style movements. Oceania laughed and tried to follow him. The TurtleBoys picked up the beat. They were creating a new style of Turtle jamming. Pots grabbed a conch shell and started to blow into it.

Doc walked over to Pots, pulled the seaweed clothing from him, and whispered, "Let's not forget that we are strangers in a strange land."

"Just having a little fun Doc!" Pots laughed.

Oceania draped the cloth back on him. Several young Dolphin girls began to dance to the strange lively music.

Corbin took Serena into his arms and they began to dance. There was a low mumbling among the crowd but Doc took Marianna into his arms, then Pots did the same with Oceania. The three couples danced to the jazzy music. As the melody played, Serena fantasized about Jaween never returning. As she danced to the music her focus became Corbin. All else faded from her sight. Her thoughts carried her to a vision of herself and Corbin floating in deep blue waters. She sensually saw herself giving him the *Kiss of Life* and wondered if it was just ancient Whale Lore or could a Mermaid's love make the miracle come true?

"Serena, promise me you will not mate with that monster Jaween." Corbin held Serena tightly.

"Corbin, you are a Lander and must one day return to your world." Serena's eyes were filled with sadness.

"I am the *Kilahara*, and I am part of your world now." Corbin pulled her closer.

There was a possessiveness about his grip. She noticed the eyes of her people watching and pulled back saying, "Corbin... what is your world like?"

He noticed her apprehension and for a moment he eased off. "Well, it's a lot noisier than here, except of course when the Dolphin girls chatter."

Corbin looked over at Pots and Oceania clicking and squealing away.

"There is the sky." Corbin looked up and eased her back into his arms. "There are stars, sunrises, sunsets, and people, lots of Landers, maybe that's not the best part. But there's chocolate and ice cream and chicken fried steak."

"Chicken fried what?" Serena smiled.

"Did you say steak?" Doc eased Marianna closer.

"We were just talking about the Lander World."

"Oh yes, and there are libraries bigger than this whole city, and universities filled with laboratories..." Doc took the opportunity to talk about his interests with Marianna.

Pots overheard and twirled Oceania around. "And jazz clubs and beer."

A MerWoman interrupted Serena and Corbin. She held up her little MerBaby. It was a baby MerGirl. She shoved the baby in Corbin's arms and chattered in Dolphin.

Corbin held up the child and looked over at Serena as if pleading for help.

"She wants to thank the *Kilahara*. She says her daughter is alive today only because of him and his magic."

Corbin held the little MerGirl up. "She's adorable." He tried to ease his discomfort.

"Isn't she precious." Serena smiled. "She hasn't even learned to separate her legs yet."

Serena tickled her under the chin and clicked a couple of times. The baby smiled then sneezed a glob of mucoid goop. It sprayed out of her mouth hitting Corbin in the face and dripped down like a jar of honey.

"Yuck." Corbin shoved the baby back into her mother's arms. He forced a smile. "Cute little sucker."

Serena laughed and wiped the glob from Corbin's face.

Doc waltzed over with Marianna. "I see that she's still *sweaning*."

"What?" Corbin wiped his face to see if it was clean.

"*Sweaning*, it's kind of like teething but a whole lot messier. May I cut in?" Doc whisked Serena away before Corbin could protest.

A tear fell from Serena's eyes as she confided in her mentor, "Doc, I can't go on like this, I want to be with him so much!"

"Just think about Jaween crushing his tiny Lander skull like a crab shell."

Serena got the message.

CHAPTER SEVENTEEN

"The plankton fields needed to be harvested daily. They were the primary source of food now for all the MerPeople, since the MerWarriors had still not returned. Corbin and I spent much time together underwater. Corbin was becoming fluent in Dolphin and we worked together well under water."

Corbin swam behind Serena. His movements were slow and clumsy compared to the swiftness and fluidity with which Serena navigated Mother Ocean. As she glided through the water, she squealed to him in Dolphin and pointed. They both dove toward a bed of seaweed.

Corbin pulled out a knife and cut some loose. Serena opened a bag and stuffed it in.

"I think that's it for today," Serena squealed. Then she pointed around him. "Those in the front pasture should be ready before long, if we cut them too soon they won't have all the proper nutrients."

Corbin sheathed his knife while Serena sorted through the bag. She looked up.

Corbin had drifted closer to her. All this time working so close to Serena and not having her had been torture. He grabbed her and pulled her behind a large coral reef. He ran his hands over her breasts. She wriggled free, dropping the bag to the ocean floor. Corbin was in pursuit. He surprised her from behind.

He placed his hands over her breasts and ran his thumbs over her nipples. Serena tried to pull back, but Corbin's passion was ignited. He held her tighter. Serena felt her body tingle with aliveness. She opened her mouth and squealed in delight. She felt desire shoot throughout her body as he ran his fingers down her stomach and around her belly button. Her body wriggled and she let out a spray of bubbles as she moaned. Corbin kept moving his fingers down until he hit the area below her navel. In the water her skin had turned to fish scales and the suckers bound her thighs tightly together. He paused, not sure of how to proceed. Serena was obviously very excited in a fishy kind of way. She flipped her great tail back and forth.

If this is the Great Whale Mother's will then let him take me now, Serena thought, as she surrendered her body to the mysterious Lander. Corbin hesitantly touched her scales. He ran his hand down toward the suckers that fastened her thighs together. She moaned with pleasure. Underwater, the suckers on Serena's tube feet were extremely active. Corbin pried her legs apart. As Serena became more excited her suckers secreted mucus. Serena kept her eyes closed and squealed, obviously finding the whole experience highly erotic.

Suddenly, the whole scene became too weird for Corbin. He jerked back, jolting Serena from her euphoric state. She opened her eyes and looked at him, suddenly becoming embarrassed of her body. A wave of shame passed through her, accompanied by a deep feeling of hurt. She quickly swam off leaving Corbin in her wake.

Serena entered the throne room. She climbed the stairs and kissed the great black pearl ring on her father's hand. He was seated on the carved coral throne.

"What is it you wish to discuss, father?" Serena looked into her father's worried eyes.

"Jaween and the MerWarriors have returned."

Serena felt a tingle of fear rush down her spine but shook it off.

"There is much talk throughout the Quams about you and this Lander. If Jaween hears of this..."

She stood up and walked over and touched her jewel-encrusted crown, which sat over the throne beside her father. "It is idle talk." Her fingers fondled the rubies and sapphires.

"Serena, you are Queen of all MerWorld. You are a direct descendant from a great line of queens!"

"Nothing has happened between me and the Lander!" Serena turned in anger.

Halstaff took the crown and placed it in her hands. "Many MerPeople have sacrificed themselves so you could ascend to the throne, so your descendants could rule. Please don't jeopardize that on an infatuation with this Lander."

Suddenly the crown felt very heavy. She thought about his words and all he and her mother had given up to insure that she would be queen. Her mind raced to the look on Corbin's face as he watched her fishy body become aroused. How revolted he was by her. It was obvious they were two very different species. She was a queen, why did she lower herself to be humiliated by a common Lander? Serena felt her heart harden as she spoke.

"Don't worry father, my crown is secure."

Halstaff, sensing the right moment had finally arrived, clasped his claw-like hand on her shoulder. "May I make the announcement that you will mate with Jaween?"

Serena's nostrils flared in disgust.

"Your words would bring great peace to these old ears."

Serena bowed her head. Halstaff leaned in. "I must speak to my mother first."

Corbin wandered into Doc's makeshift laboratory. He picked up a book on biology and kicked back on the bunk, flipping through the pages while Doc examined something under the microscope. Corbin opened the book to the page on fish anatomy. He crumpled his nose as he looked at a picture of a fish fertilizing eggs.

"Doc, do you know anything about how fish...you know... do it?" Corbin asked. Doc looked up from the microscope and rubbed his tired eyes, then glanced at the picture.

"Really Corbin, I thought you were above pornography."

"You know Doc, I haven't felt this way since...Rachel."

"Yeah, well, forget it! In case you haven't noticed our situation is a bit precarious. We're approximately five hundred feet under the ocean's surface, in an extremely hostile environment."

"What do you mean hostile? The MerPeople love us, I'm the *Kilahara* and you're their miracle healer."

"Jaween hates your guts, if you haven't noticed!" Doc poured a strange green substance into a test tube.

"I haven't seen him around lately."

"Not to mention the fact that our race is systematically exterminating their race."

"You don't know that for a fact."

"Meanwhile, you're trying to get it on with their mermaid queen." Doc held up the test tube and examined it.

"MerMaiden, thank you!"

Pots walked in. "You mean you still haven't done it yet?"

"And you have?" Corbin sat up.

Pots grinned. "Every day and twice on Sundays." Pots leaned over Doc. "Hey, you done with that stuff yet?"

"Almost." Doc looked up. "You see the problem with you, Corbin, is that you're a racist."

Corbin laughed, "A racist?"

"Mmm, and a snob." Doc poured the contents of the test tube back into a boiling pot of green gook.

"Gee, don't hold back, Doc, give it to me straight." Corbin looked over at Pots. "Pots, do you think I'm a racist?"

"Permission to speak freely, Captain?" Pots smiled

"Okay...uh, yeah." Corbin shook his head at his insubordinate crew.

"Well, I wouldn't call you a racist, or bigot, or anything like that, let's just say you're a bit close-minded."

"Close-minded?" Corbin shouted.

"And maybe a bit of a prude." Pots thought carefully, then looked at the mixture Doc was smelling.

"Well put, Pots." Doc dipped a spoon in and tasted it.

"Thank you, Doc."

"Hold on just a doggone minute you two. Before you go sizing me up I'd like to say a thing or two in my defense. I'm about the most open-minded...you mean just because I want my girlfriend to look...normal?"

Doc looked at Pots and raised his eyebrows. "Normal?" He stared at Corbin. "This may sound strange to you, but did you ever stop to think that maybe Serena finds your anatomy a bit weird?"

"You have to learn to appreciate women for their uniqueness." Pots grinned. "For example, some men might think a small roll of fat around the middle is unattractive. But I find a little poundage on a woman gives me something extra I can hold onto." Pots made a kind of comical thrusting motion.

"That's not fair! Now you know Pots would hump a sea walrus if we were stranded in the Arctic!" Corbin protested.

"I don't know if I could stand the competition. Did you know that a male walrus has the second largest..."

"Okay Pots, you made your point. So how did you make your way past those little..." Corbin puckered his face, "little... sucker things."

"Actually, those tube feet suckers become highly sensitive to a MerWoman when she is submerged. In fact, they take on a highly sexual role in the underwater mating ritual," Doc calmly explained.

"Et tu, Brute, Doc?" Corbin grimaced. "With Marianna?"

Doc smiled, "You haven't really done it until you've had MerSex."

"Imagine hundreds of tiny little clitoris spreading out before you!" Pots made a little sucker sound with his mouth that turned Corbin's stomach.

"Oh come on! You guys are sick!" Corbin threw the book down.

"Hey don't forget about *Wa Aloo!*" Pots smiled a shit-eating grin.

"*Wa Aloo?*" Corbin's face was blank.

"Boy, have you been missing out!" Pots chuckled.

Corbin looked over to Doc for an explanation. "*Wa Aloo?*"

Doc continued, "Dolphin Girls who meet the proper requirements," Pots snickered as Doc quieted him with a scholarly glare, "are taken to the temple of Poseidon and trained in the ancient art of *Wa Aloo*."

"What's *Wa Al...*" an immediate understanding passed through Corbin's face.

"Oh...That's...that's sacrilegious!"

"Well, I rest my case!" Doc smiled. "I'm glad we had this little talk. It helps to put things into perspective."

"But in a temple, for God's sake!"

"In the days of the ancient Whale Women, MerSex was not only a means of propagation but of a way of merging with Mother Ocean. They transcended their consciousness as they achieved the ultimate climax. Kind of a microcosmic big bang theory in reverse." Doc put his glasses back on and poured the strange substance back into the test tube. He held the test tube up and inspected it, then drank it down. "Perfect." He gasped.

"Well, grab that stuff and come on!" Pots rushed up the ladder. Doc took a pot of the solution and followed.

"Hey, where are you two off to?" Corbin called out.

"Oh, Oceania and Marianna are in the Jacuzzi waiting for us." Doc smiled and followed Pots up the ladder.

Corbin laid back down on his cot, "Great, everybody's getting laid except me!"

CHAPTER EIGHTEEN

Oh Mother Ocean, why do the Landers not see
That they are robbing the life force
From the depths of your sea.
No matter how many signs you send them
They continue to ignore
Are they so deaf, dumb and stupid
They cannot hear disaster knocking at their door?
So many of your creatures have already given up and died
How much deeper in the ocean must we all go to hide?
There is no more escape from the poisons they have given me
I shall give up my soul to the Great Whale Mother,
Ruler of the Sea.

Much water had passed and Serena had not felt her mother's presence in quite some time. She had missed her greatly but with the spreading sickness and famine she could not leave her people in their greatest hour of need. Sensing that something was wrong, Serena slipped out of the Gates of Mer and swam to the spot where she had first met the apparition those many seasons ago. Serena floated peacefully, emptying her mind from all the worldly cares of Corbin, her people, Jaween and her father. Her mind drifted back to her mother's teachings, the wonders of her Spirit Quest and her amazing encounter with Shamana, the last of the Ocean Keepers. So much had happened since then, but still she had not found her own life current. If it wasn't with the Lander than why would Mother Ocean not give him back to his world? She must ask her mother these questions.

A cloaked figure appeared in the shadow of the reef.

"Where is my mother?" Serena's Whale Song showed concern.

"I will take you to her." The figure set out for the Mariana Trench. Serena followed as closely as she could.

She swam past the familiar islands to the point where the waters became calm. Then down she plummeted into the underwater world of the Abyss. Serena followed the woman into the darkness, then into the winding corridors until she stopped at an opening.

The old whale woman motioned for Serena to enter. She swam into the cave. Once inside she noticed an area where the water drew back. There, resting upon a bed of seaweed, lay Chaila. Serena went to her. She could see she was ill.

"Mother." Tears filled Serena's eyes as she looked into her mother's face and noticed it was pale and her lips were blue. "What's wrong?" She stroked her mother's hair.

"The water of my life has run out." Chaila strained to speak.

"Mother, I can't bear to lose you again!" Serena sobbed in her mother's bosom.

"I'm sorry, but when the Great Whale Mother calls, you must come." Chaila forced herself to speak but was very weak.

"Lie still,"...Serena was interrupted by her mother's gentle touch.

"Serena, you must know the truth about your father..." Chaila clutched her daughter's hand as she struggled to speak. In all the time they had been together she had rarely heard her mother's soft melodious voice, except raised in Whale Song. It was a beautiful voice, so gentle and loving. She longed to hear more of it.

"My father?" Serena strained to hear her mother's words.

"Yes, you and Jaween are..." Chaila struggled to finish her final words but her breath left her, never to return.

Serena clutched her mother's lifeless body wishing for more, more time, more tenderness, more of the mother's love she had so desperately longed for as a child. But there was no more time. A deluge of tears fell from Serena's eyes. Tears she had never felt before. She stayed there all through the night clinging to her mother's body as it grew cold and stiff. At last, after what seemed like many seasons, the ocean of tears inside of her subsided. She gently pulled her mother's lifeless body into the deep waters. She dragged her mother through a myriad of tunnels. A group of Whale Women appeared in the openings of each corridor holding fluorescent lights as if to honor her mother's passing. Then Serena realized they were also honoring her. They bowed as she passed.

Serena dragged her mother's limp body, her clothing billowing behind her, through the dark tunnels and into the brilliant glow of crystalline walls. She drew in a breath as she swam toward the brilliant white light emanating from the Portal of Time. She remembered her mother's stringent warning about the power of the Portal, but she felt compelled to move toward it, wanting to see her mother's body all the way to the other side.

She reached the opening into the Portal of Time and stared, mesmerized by the pulsating waves of energy that rippled in front of her. She stared into it, hypnotized by its immense power, until she noticed a pair of penetrating blue eyes, much like her own, staring back from the other side. In an instant, an amazing charge of electrical energy reached out and pulled her mother's body into the vortex. Serena felt herself being uncontrollably pulled in by the magnitude of the suction. She clawed at the tunnel walls, groping for something to stop her from being pulled through. The energy tugged at her like a whirlpool, her grip slipped, and she was about to follow her mother to her death when she felt a strong arm pushing her back from the Abyss. She found herself flung out of the whirlpool's grip and back on the other side. The Portal had shut. Peaceful ripples once again returned. The surge of energy cleared and Serena saw her mother alive on the other side, and beside her, a handsome young MerWarrior. He had long jet black hair and piercing blue eyes just like Serena's. He touched his hand to his lips and sent Serena a kiss. He turned to Chaila and they kissed one another, then disappeared. For a moment Serena felt compelled to swim after them, but she heard her mother's voice clearly in her mind...

Serena, now is not your time. You must find your own life current. Serena pulled herself back.

I will always be with you. Chaila's words echoed in Serena's mind. She felt great comfort in her words. She swam up toward the light of the pale blue waters. The heaviness of her heart was gone. She was filled with the joy of knowing that her mother was all right and on the other side of the Abyss.

"I remember thinking, *who was that dark MerWarrior floating beside my mother and what was it she was about to tell me about myself and Jaween?* A deluge of disturbing emotions tugged at my mind as I fought the deep waters. A gnawing thought penetrated my mind but I pushed it back into the deep recesses of my heart, afraid to hear its truth. All I wanted now was to return to the familiarity of the surface world. There everything was as it should be.

I broke through the surface waters and felt the warmth of the sun shining on my face. It felt good to be alive. I looked around at the gentle waves of Mother Ocean and felt a gentle breeze kiss my cheek. Then the pungent smell of dead fish hit my nostrils. Nausea arose in my stomach. I looked around and noticed schools of dead fish bobbing in the waves. My instincts told me to dive deep and swim away from the poisonous waters. I quickly swam toward MerWorld. As I swam I thought about the sickness my mother contracted.

Was it the same sickness? If only I had come earlier, maybe I could have treated her with the sacred serum Doc and I had created. Or perhaps my mother had succumbed to the sickness when I had not returned from my Spirit Quest. *Did my mother leave the safety of the Abyss in search of me?* Suddenly I felt a strange urge to seek comfort in Corbin's strong arms, the last place I should go."

CHAPTER NINETEEN

Jaween was hidden behind the coral reef. His claw-like hand shot out and quickly closed on his victim's throat. Ios looked up into Jaween's evil eyes.

"Do you have some news for me?"

"I have been watching them closely..." Ios gasped.

"Did Serena and that Lander..." Jaween's eyes were bulging and his nostrils flared. His grip tightened around Ios's neck as he stared off in a blind jealous rage.

"No! No," Ios gurgled. "She is only working to find a cure for the sickness with the healer."

"You lie!" Jaween hit him hard against his head. Then again. Ios felt his life force leaving him.

"How does this healer know what to do for our people?" Jaween shook the old man's fragile body. "Well. Say it old Turtle, or I'll tear you in two!"

"He believes that his Lander Quam has caused all our problems. He feels responsible."

At last, I have something I can use! Jaween smiled and let the limp body of Ios fall from his grip. Ios lay dying on the ocean floor as Jaween swam away to confer with his mother.

Sharfina had grown too fat and lazy to propel her own body weight, so her bodyguards had to pull her around in a carved coral carriage. She was returning from her visit with Halstaff, where she had once more been unsuccessful in pressing him to announce the mating of Serena with her son. Upset by the latest delay, she decided she would not rest until she saw the blood of that Lander darken the waters of Mer.

She had decided to incite her son against the Lander and end his life once and for all. The only question was how to arouse his temper without endangering herself.

Two of her escorts kneeled beneath Sharfina so she could step across their backs as she left her carriage of carved coral and entered her private bubble chamber. Her chamber was richly decorated with many of the spoils from the reign of Queen Chat'an. There was the treasure chest that had at one time sat at the foot of Queen Chat'an's great coral bed, along with many other trinkets from her royal bedchamber.

She delighted in the inlaid seashell arrangements that covered most of her furniture. She had a peculiar affection for turtle shell. Everything she owned was made of the rare commodity. Hand-carved turtle shell combs lay upon Sharfina's dressing table. She especially loved whole polished carcasses, which she used as washbasins or cushioned with seaweed to create sitting stools. She hunted sea turtles with a passion. She also made it a point of giving King Halstaff presents of them. Under MerEtiquette, it was considered highly offensive for a Quam to use another Quam's totem or animal artifacts. For example, the Dolphin Quam used dolphin artifacts out of respect for the power they gave their people, just as the Shark Quam used shark hide, shark oil and shark teeth and made presents of them at their own discretion. But for Sharfina, half Shark and half Dolphin, it was a sacrilege to use the sacred Turtle in this fashion and even worse to present them as gifts to a member of the Turtle Quam.

Sharfina gazed out over the dome section of the city she had ordered to be set aside for the Brotherhood of the Shark. When she became High Priestess she had acquired these large chambers along with other spoils of war, but eventually her authority was no longer respected by the Shark Quam. They cast her and her laws out, making up their own rules. She had condemned them all as blasphemers and receded into a hermitic existence. She had retained a handful of MerWarriors as her personal bodyguards by her rights as mother of Jaween and mate of Triton. She still managed to intimidate Halstaff with her feeble display of power.

Today Jaween was late and she was growing hungry for her

portion of fish and octopus. She dismissed her bodyguards for privacy's sake and let her anger fester. At last Jaween entered her bubbled sanctum.

"I thought the whales would return before you showed your ungrateful hide! What have you brought me, you miserable spawn?" Sharfina was quite annoyed as she ripped open his seaweed sack to find his spoils. "Is this all you bring?" Sharfina pulled out a fish and ripped its head off with her sharp shark teeth.

"Be grateful for what you have, old Shark Woman. The ocean waters give forth little. They are filled only with death and decay." Jaween lived for these precious moments when his mother fueled his hopes of mating with Serena. It was true that most of what she said she fabricated to serve her own selfish needs, but at least he had something to hang onto. However, today she was unusually angry and sick of eating plankton.

"What news of Serena?" Jaween could scarcely contain himself.

"There is much news my son, but since you have not brought me one single squid, I shall have to save it for another time."

Jaween knew his mother all too well. "Very well." Jaween reached into his pouch and pulled out a squid.

"Squid!" Sharfina smiled and drool ran down her black lips. She slurped the creature up, then crushed it to death between her razor sharp teeth.

"Now, tell me everything!" Jaween interrupted her feast.

"Oh my son, I am afraid the news is not good!" Sharfina slurped up the tentacles that hung from her mouth. Ink stains dripped down her cheeks.

"In the name of Poseidon, Mother, speak!" Jaween grunted in Shark.

Sharfina decided to risk angering Jaween because it was time to change her current situation, time for Jaween to make his move.

"Is Serena in trouble?" Jaween voiced a sincere concern.

"Of the worst kind, she has been seduced by that, that Lander!"

Jaween's face turned blue; he grabbed his mother by the throat. "You lie!"

Sharfina struggled to breathe. "It's true. Two of the Dolphin girls saw them, they were mating, by the right of water!"

"By the right of water, but how?"

"There is talk of a mating ritual between the two of them! Of him becoming king!" Sharfina knew she was spreading lies but she was bored with her life and wanted to move into the palace.

"Son, our blood line is at risk! And your crown!"

Jaween gasped for air. His face turned deep blue.

I must steer his anger toward the Lander and away from me, Sharfina thought.

"My son, you must kill this Lander!" Sharfina grunted out in Shark.

"Yes!" He gnashed his sharp teeth and dove through the bubble wall. Sharfina smiled, pleased with herself. At last she would have her position of authority restored.

Corbin took another swig of green juice. "You know after about the eleventh one you really can't taste the difference."

"What difference?" Doc and Pots had returned to the sub to find Corbin smashed.

"The difference between this and gin."

"This doesn't taste anything like gin," Doc commented

"That's what I mean." Corbin got up and stumbled over to the ship's control. He pushed a button and the battle station alert sounded. Corbin slurred his words as he swaggered over to the intercom. He pulled it down and slobbered into it, "Now hear this, now hear this, battle stations, battle stations."

Doc took the intercom from him and turned off the alarm.

"I miss doing that shit! Hey, you think we could blast our way out of here?" Corbin shouted.

"Come on Cap, I think you better lie down for a bit." Doc looked at Pots. "We've got to sober him up."

Doc put his arm over Corbin's shoulder and helped him sit down.

Pots started to brew some seaweed coffee. "So where are our MerWomen?"

There was an ungodly tapping sound that echoed through the sub.

"Uh oh! Sounds like we may have some trouble." Pots and Doc listened. The tapping was growing louder and moved around the sub.

"Come on Jaween!I'll kill-a-hara you right now!" Corbin cried out and tried to stand.

"Shush!" Doc pushed Corbin back down. "That's Marianna."

"How do you know that?" Pots asked.

"Because I taught her Morse code. Go on open the hatch." Doc motioned to Pots.

Marianna and Oceania climbed into the sub.

"Jaween and his MerWarriors are back and they want blood!" Marianna squealed out in Dolphin.

Doc flipped a switch on to electrify the deck as a safety precaution. "This may slow them down."

"Yeah, fry those fish heads!" Corbin mumbled.

"What's wrong with him?" Marianna squealed.

"He's plastered," Doc responded.

"Now, what's wrong with this Jaween guy?" Corbin tried to stand up but found himself flat on the floor. "What did we ever do to him anyway?"

Doc rolled his eyes and he and Pots both picked Corbin up.

Just then a huge seaquake rocked the submarine.

"I had just made my way through the opening of the cave into MerWorld when the ocean floor shook with a tremendous force. I watched as the massive boulders that had blocked the entrance for so many seasons shook loose and hurtled down upon MerWorld. I did my best to dodge them as they rained down upon me. This was by far the strongest seaquake I had ever felt. Schools of fish scattered. Corals splintered and fell from their beds. Debris stirred up a cloud so thick that I could not see what was in front of me. Then came the sound. It was an intense low sound, as if it had been carried many fathoms through the sea. I had never heard a sound of this magnitude.

Great Mother of Whales, what could it be? I thought, as I batted my hands in front of my face trying to stop the sand from getting into my eyes. The huge boulders fell upon my city, penetrating the great bubble dome walls. I tried to swim toward the Gates of MerWorld but I was lost in a whirlpool of MerPeople swimming for their lives. The whole city was in a panic. I felt myself being trampled in the wake of the frantic MerPeople. I was pushed farther and farther away from the gates; the more I struggled, the more I was pushed away. Finally, exhausted to the point where I could swim no more, I let myself drift to the bottom. It was then I felt Jaween's mighty arms holding me tightly about my waist. He carried me to the palace. I was too weak to protest.

Inside the Great Amphitheater frightened MerPeople had gathered seeking safety, peace of mind and answers from their king. But my Halstaff only sat on his throne, shaking. He cowered inside his turtle shell armor, obviously at a loss of words to explain the most recent calamity. Jaween burst through the bubble dome wall. He climbed the stairs that ascended to the thrones with me in his arms. The MerPeople became silent. I was too exhausted to speak. I tried to free myself but Jaween's grip was too tight."

"My King, my people, once again I have delivered your queen from the jaws of death." Jaween knew this was his moment to dispel the *Kilahara* myth and rid himself of this Lander once and for all. He turned to the desperate Quams.

A MerWoman from one of the Quams cried out, "Jaween, I am frightened! What are these seaquakes that are plaguing our waters?"

Another MerWoman cried out, "Jaween, I have lost my only child!"

An old TurtleMan cried out also, "In my region my entire Quam is gone!"

"Jaween, we want answers." A solo voice echoed and then the entire crowd joined in.

Serena looked at the crowd. It was a blur. She wanted to stand up and tell her people to remain calm. But her body was too weak from the struggle and her long swim from the Abyss.

"It is the wrath of Poseidon!" Jaween bellowed out. The Quams were quiet; a few MerWomen gasped.

"What have we done to anger our Lord Poseidon?" an old MerWoman cried out.

"You have taken this unholy Lander as your *Kilahara* and worshiped him over Poseidon and the Shark God himself."

Sharfina had arrived in her carriage drawn by her bodyguards, just in time to catch her son's words. *Brilliant, my son, brilliant, praise be to the Shark God. I hold the reigns to his power with my secret. Or he may overpower even me*, Sharfina thought.

"I have just learned that it is the Landers who are destroying our waters, killing our fish and blasting our homes. Just as the Great Queen Chat'an predicted when she moved us to the safety of this cave. But what have you infidels done? You have taken the enemy into your bosom! You have placed him above your Lord Poseidon. When was the last time you entered the Temple of Poseidon and made sacrifices?" Jaween stared into the scared faces of the crowd.

"What must we do to appease Poseidon so he will protect us against these evil Landers?" a MerWarrior cried out.

Serena lifted her head. She wanted to sing out in Whale

Song but only a raspy sound came from her throat. Jaween looked down at her and whispered, "If you value the life of your Lander you will be still."

Serena collapsed her head against Jaween's great chest.

"But Poseidon cannot blame you, my people. The evil of the Landers is great! Why, this Lander has bewitched you into thinking he is the *Kilahara*. He has even seduced our queen into postponing our mating." Jaween looked down into Serena's eyes and spoke softly, while the Quam cheered, "It's all right, My Queen, I forgive you."

All Serena could see was Corbin's face in front of her. It was filled with disgust as he gazed at her strange anatomy. *The quake has removed the rubble. He can leave now. You and Jaween, those were the dying words of my mother. It must be the Will of Mother Ocean. It must be,* Serena thought.

"Death to the Landers!" A cry rang out from deep within Sharfina's throat and soon the desperate Quams had attached themselves to the idea. Serena looked up into Jaween's cold eyes. He was excited. His breathing became fast and strained.

"Tonight you will become my mate," Jaween whispered into Serena's ear.

"The passage is free, you must let the Landers leave, unharmed." Serena struggled to speak.

Jaween smiled at Serena in a way that made her body shiver. "Then we have a bargain?"

Serena nodded, then closed her eyes and slipped into darkness.

"We must not destroy these Landers." As Jaween spoke there was a sigh of disappointment. "We must send them back to where they came from with a message!" Jaween yelled. The crowd cheered.

"But enough about the cursed Landers, tonight we will celebrate their departure with a mating ritual between your queen and myself."

The Quams broke into cheers. They began chanting, "Jaween, Jaween, Jaween!"

Sharfina gloated. Jaween had worked his magic. Gone were their fears. MerWorld was filled with the hope of the new union.

Doc and Pots embraced their MerWomen for the last time on the shore beside the sub. They had been given the news and accepted their fate. Now the only chore was to tell Corbin.

Tears filled Marianna's eyes as she silently gave the sign of the Turtle to Doc and the unsaid understanding was transmitted telepathically between the two of them. It was the knowledge that what they were doing was for a higher good.

Oceania and Pots, on the other hand, blubbered away with gusto.

"I'll never forget you baby! Never!" Pots promised.

Doc had heard him utter those words before on countless cruises, but somehow this time Doc believed he meant it.

Oceania squealed a mournful tune as the two sailors boarded their sub.

Corbin was sitting quietly in the galley. Doc handed him his fifth cup of coffee.

"So apparently the seaquake shook the rubble loose. We're free to leave." Doc tried to soften the blow.

"Who told you that?" Corbin set down his cup.

"The MerWarriors paid us a visit," Pots answered.

"Where's Serena?" Corbin stood up. "What happened to Serena?" Corbin looked into their faces.

"They gave us an ultimatum, either we take our big fish and go home or else." Doc looked at Corbin.

"Well it looks like it's time to go home." Pots began to put things away.

"Home! We can't...wait, what about Serena?" Corbin frowned. "We're not going anywhere without Serena!"

"Look, all of MerWorld has been shaken up by this last blast, they're not kidding this time. Jaween has managed to stir the whole city up against us." Doc added, "And there's more."

"What?" Corbin looked up.

Doc softly put his hand on Corbin's shoulder. "Serena's mating with Jaween...tonight."

Corbin threw his tin cup at the wall. "It's not true!"

"It was her decision." Doc sighed.

Corbin looked into Doc's kind and all-knowing eyes. He recognized his tone. "It can't be true."

"It's time to go home." Doc spoke softly.

"Home?" Corbin looked up as if awaking from a dream.

CHAPTER TWENTY

Serena stood beside Jaween in the great dome bubble reciting her mating vows as Corbin's submarine squeezed through the small opening, leaving MerWorld behind. Serena's hair was slicked back with shark oil and braided into tiny tight knots. Never again would Serena be permitted to wander through the ocean with her long blonde curls gently tossing about in the current.

"Does the Queen Serena promise to respect, honor and obey her Master and Lord Jaween, son of Triton, son of Poseidon, all the days of her life?" The old Shark Priest muttered.

Serena inhaled the stench of the shark oil; it reminded her of that day many seasons ago when the Great Whale Mother had heard her pleas and sent Corbin to her rescue in his great steel beast. Serena did not even attempt to call upon the Whale Mother now. She had found her life current. *It was the will of Mother Ocean, it must be,* Serena thought.

"I will." Serena agreed to what seemed more like a prison term than a mating call.

"The priest can't hear you, my pet," Jaween whispered.

"I promise to obey him," Serena grunted forth in vulgar Shark.

"Soon all your regrets will be quieted when I plunge my mighty spear into you. Then you will live only to bring me pleasure!"

The old priest bound Serena to Jaween's wrists with seaweed strands. "As I bind your hands, so do I bind your lives. By Poseidon, Ruler of the Sea, you are now joined together one life to the other until the day you cease to exist. Now go forth and consummate the union."

Serena lay in the center of a seaweed bed with only the thin traditional woven seaweed veil to cover her nakedness. Oceania and Marianna had carefully prepared her in the ancient way to receive her mate's sacred seed; then and only then would she be mated with Jaween for life. With the sacred exchange of virginal blood and holy MerMan semen, the union would be complete. She watched the whale oil lamp flicker as she trembled at the idea of Jaween plunging his mighty trident into her the way she had seen him do to the great whites, over and over again.

Jaween was also being prepared in the traditional way by his mother, who rubbed shark oil over his muscular body. He sat impatiently as his mother stroked him in a seductive way.

"Hurry mother! Serena awaits me!" Jaween was gasping for air.

Sharfina took her time rubbing the oil into his chest and down his legs close to his large spear, sensing his arousal. Her jealousy was rising.

"Just like your father, so impatient to mate with a Whale Woman whore!" Sharfina whispered. Her anger was only subdued by the knowledge that her moment of revenge was close at hand. All those years of waiting and conspiring were about to pay off! Now she was going to let out the truth she had so carefully guarded.

"What are you muttering about old woman?" Jaween grunted.

"I said you remind me of your father rushing off to mate with Chaila; he never loved me and you never loved me either! You think tonight you will finally be rid of me. Don't you?" Sharfina's nostrils flared as she ran to her treasure chest and pulled out a box. "Here, my son, a gift for you." She held out the box and gave it to him. Jaween grunted.

"I don't want your gifts old Shark Woman, I don't want anything more from you! I have Serena now!"

"Open the box, son. This gift is for Serena."

Jaween opened the lid of the finely carved turtle shell jewelry box. Inside lay half of a broken emerald heart suspended from a chain. Jaween picked it up.

"Serena's heart, where did you find it?" Jaween took it in his hands and examined it. "This will make a fine mating gift."

"Give it to her, and see the surprise on her face, my son, for this is not her heart but yours, given to you by her mother Chaila, many seasons ago."

Jaween looked confused.

"I have been saving it, all these seasons, for this special night."

"Old woman, I grow impatient!"

"Chaila gave each half of the famed broken Emerald Heart of the Sea to each of you."

"Why would a Whale Woman do that?"

"Because she wanted brother and sister to recognize one another when they grew up."

"Brother and sister?" Jaween wrestled to understand.

"Do what you like tonight to relieve yourself my son, but do not plant your seed inside Serena because *she* is your sister!"

Jaween's face turned blue with rage. "NOOOOOO!" He cried out as he clutched the necklace. "It is not true! You told me my father died so his heirs would sit on the throne!"

"And they will, since Serena is his daughter."

"But you lied to me!"

Sharfina smiled.

Jaween took the necklace he held in his hands and wrapped it around his mother's neck. "And you are lying now!" Jaween grunted out, as he squeezed the necklace's chain around Sharfina's fat neck. She tried to scream for her bodyguards but all that escaped was her fat, inky, black tongue that flapped outside her mouth and a low guttural grunt punctuated by

Jaween's gasps for air. Sharfina's face turned the same dark shade of blue as her son's. Jaween squeezed the last bit of life from the woman who had given life to him.

Serena's thoughts turned to Corbin as she lay trembling, naked and vulnerable beneath the thin seaweed sheet. *Great Whale Mother, please let Corbin make it safely out of MerWorld and away from Jaween and his MerWarriors. Let him be reunited with his Lander family and find happiness.*

Serena noticed the shadow of towering muscles approaching her through the drapes that enclosed the nuptial bed. The shadow flickered against the curtains as the whale oil lamp burnt low. She smelled the strong aroma of the fresh shark oil and heard Jaween's gasping breath.

Jaween pulled back the curtain. His body glistened as the shark oil reflected in the lamp's glow, revealing his rippling muscles.

"I have a wedding gift for you, my pet." Jaween smiled, revealing his blackened pointy Shark teeth. He held up the half of the broken Emerald Heart.

Serena looked shocked. "Where did you get this?"

Jaween clasped it around her neck. "I see it surprises you?" Jaween looked into her eyes. "You thought you had lost it forever."

"But..." Serena tried to speak.

Jaween gently covered her mouth with a seaweed gag. "Don't speak, my pet. I know it isn't customary," Jaween tied her hands and feet with seaweed bonds to the four post bed; he licked her ear as he whispered into it, "but I must stop your Whale Woman voice. Too bad you cannot enjoy the taste of me in your mouth!"

Serena tried to stop him but he had already secured her.

"Many a MerMaiden would be filled with joy to be chosen by the great Chief MerWarrior himself."

Jaween whispered softly in her ear. Serena's naked body trembled under the thin veil. He looked down at her voluptuous body with only the thin mating sheet separating him from his prize.

"At last! All those seasons of waiting patiently, now you are mine." Savoring her beautiful naked body he extended his callous finger under the sheet and rubbed it over her nipple. Serena tried to cry out but the gag stopped her enchanting voice.

She was in his bed, not the Lander's. She would bear his seed; his sacred linage would rule MerWorld. Jaween's thoughts tried to block out the lies his mother had told him! *After all, the old Shark Woman was dead!* He pulled down the sheet, slowly exposing Serena's beautiful breasts, taking his time to savor her like a dessert. He ran his long tongue around her nipples. Serena struggled and pulled on the ropes but Jaween only laughed.

"Now I will plunge my mighty spear into you making you mine forever." He thrust his long tongue into her ear.

She struggled to free herself but could not. She closed her eyes and offered a silent prayer once again to the Great Whale Mother, *Oh Great Whale Mother, please, please help me!* Serena waited to feel her virginal cavity ripped open by Jaween's mighty spear, but she felt nothing. She kept her eyes closed and continued to pray.

Jaween reached for his weapon, ready to thrust it inside her bringing her into submission, but he felt only limpness, like a dead sea snake. He grabbed hold of it, grunting as he tried to shove it inside her hoping to make her his, to feel her body undulating with the pleasure only the Chief of all MerWarriors could give with his sacred staff. But Jaween could not rid his mind of his dead mother and her torturous words: *She is your sister!* Sharfina's voice echoed inside Jaween's mind. *Your sister!*

Serena opened her eyes and looked at Jaween.

"NO!" Jaween cried out as he stood up with his hands over his ears. "It's a lie!" He screamed as he gasped for air and pushed his way into the outer chamber where Mako and Bile were standing guard.

"My lord." Mako beat his chest and grunted, immediately restraining Halstaff who was trying to enter the bedchamber.

"Jaween, what are you doing? Didn't your mother tell you?" Halstaff was surprised Sharfina had permitted the mating ritual to go this far.

"Lies! You both speak lies!" Jaween wrapped his hands around the old man's throat to stop him from speaking the truth. He turned to Mako and Bile.

"Have your pleasure with this Lander whore. She has ruined herself and is not fit for my sacred staff!"

"NO!" Halstaff gasped but Jaween tightened his grip.

"Make sure there is virginal blood and holy sperm on the mating sheets for all the Quams to see." Jaween pushed Halstaff into a corner. "And tell no one what has happened here tonight."

Serena lay bound and gagged on the bed under the thin seaweed sheet. The MerWarriors walked over to Serena. They stared at her voluptuous body tied to the bed. Lust gleamed in their eyes. They smiled at one another and grunted like two ravenous Sharks ready to attack.

Outside Jaween beat Halstaff with his mighty fist. The old TurtleMan stumbled backwards as tears filled his eyes.

"Jaween, I beg you, kill me, but do not do this thing to your sister!"

"Liar!" Jaween struck the old man a powerful blow on the side of his head. Halstaff hurled to the ground. "I can't stop the MerMen before they've drained themselves. It wouldn't be...polite."

Halstaff lay on his back dying as Jaween plunged through the bubble wall to quiet his rage.

How could I have been such a fool, everything I have done was to insure Serena's safety. How could I have been so stupid as to trust a Shark? Halstaff's thoughts echoed through his mind as he strained for his last breaths.

When the MerWarriors had finally achieved complete satisfaction and exhausted themselves, they fell asleep beside Serena. Tears spilled from Serena's eyes as blood bathed her thighs. She felt the gentle hands of Marianna loosening her gag and Oceania unfastening her hands and feet.

Serena sat up. "My father?"

Marianna motioned for her to be quiet. Mako grunted and rolled over. Oceania and Marianna helped Serena up and covered her bruised body. She winced with pain as they helped her out of the chamber.

Outside the door Serena saw her father lying on the floor. Tears filled Serena's eyes as she bent over him and wept. She kissed his forehead and raised his old Turtle head up and looked into his eyes.

"Father." Serena rubbed her hands together ready to send healing energy to her loved one.

Halstaff opened his eyes. "No! I forbid it."

"But Father, you are dying!" Serena pleaded with tears in her eyes. Halstaff turned and looked out at the kingdom.

"There is nothing left to live for. My life current has run out." The old TurtleMan turned to Serena as he spoke. "And now with my last breath I must tell you the truth." Halstaff sighed. "Serena, I am not your father."

"What do you mean?" Serena looked down on his weary face.

"Chaila and I were mated in ceremony only, nothing more."

"But then...who is my father?"

"Triton, son of Poseidon, mate of Sharfina and lover to your mother."

Serena grabbed the emerald necklace around her neck. "Then Jaween is my brother?"

"Your mother gave each of you half of the necklace so you would recognize one another when you were grown. So this would not happen." Halstaff groaned and took in a deep breath. "I should have told you long ago."

"Lie still." Serena sobbed.

"I thought your mother would tell you but when she didn't...I couldn't."

Tears flooded Serena's eyes. All she could feel was compassion for this old TurtleMan who had always been there for her. "I will always think of you as my father." Serena smiled into Halstaff's wrinkled eyes. "Not some loathsome Shark!"

"Forgive me, my daughter." Halstaff smiled through his tears and let go of his last breath.

Serena held the empty shell of her father in her arms. She wanted to weep until her pain was gone. Her body ached from the brutal rape and her soul grieved the loss of everyone whom she had ever loved. Her father, her mother, even Corbin. She was alone, alone in Shark-infested waters.

Marianna pulled at Serena. "Serena, you must leave before Jaween returns!"

"It's not safe for you here." Oceania held back her tears.

Serena heard the MerWarriors stir. She nodded and pulled the two women dearest to her close. The three women held back their tears, then Serena gathered her last bit of strength and dove through the bubble wall. She swam past the Gates of Mer through the enlarged cave opening and into the open sea. She knew she had to try and make it to the Abyss, there the Whale Women would care for her. She did not know if she would make it, but she had to try.

Mako and Bile were waking up from their flesh feast. They looked around, realizing Jaween's prize was gone. They grunted to one another.

"Where did she go?" Bile grunted to Mako.

"I don't know, but Jaween will feed us to the sharks if we don't return her," Mako grunted back.

Just then Marianna ran into the room wailing and holding the bed sheet dripping in blood. Oceania followed her.

"Oh My Queen, My Queen!" Oceania let forth the deluge of tears she had been holding back.

"Where is she?" Mako stood up and reached for his dagger but it was gone.

"She has passed to the other side of the Abyss. You disgraced her so she took her own life!" Oceania wailed. And held up the bloody dagger and the bloody seaweed sheet.

"The rest of her lies in the belly of a shark!"

CHAPTER TWENTY-ONE

It was a beautiful afternoon on the island of Bikini. A balmy tropical breeze rustled through the coconut trees as the natives were herded off the island and into navy transports scheduled to take them to the neighboring islands, where they would become refugees.

Why was this happening? John thought to himself as he extended a hand to a newly evicted mother and the infant still nursing at her breast. He was a handsome young man, all of eighteen. He had Corbin's muscular build and dark brooding eyes, but the rest of him was pure Rachel.

If they were in the path of a deadly typhoon and I was whisking the mother and child to safety, maybe I could understand. But to deliberately take them from their homes to destroy their tropical paradise, it just doesn't make sense!

A brilliantly colored parrot landed on the branch of a coconut palm. A lizard crawled across the soft warm sand. All of these creatures would be dead in just a few short hours, obliterated from the face of the earth. And what of the radiation, how long would that last? John had heard rumors that the fallout would make the parts of the island that survived uninhabitable for generations.

The small child began to cry and John found himself making faces to try and raise a smile. But it was futile, even the infant knew he was getting a raw deal. *How many times have white men come to distant parts of the globe and taken the land away from countless indigenous groups? How many times would this endless cycle continue?*

John thought of his father's face, filled with concern. *Damn, if only he didn't have to lie to him.* When Corbin had gone down with his ship some ten years ago, John had grieved and accepted the fact he would never see his father again. But now that he had returned, he found the values his grandfather, Admiral Greer, had instilled in him just didn't make sense anymore.

Admiral Greer stood on the deck of the destroyer and peered out of his binoculars. The last of the boats were returning to the ship.

"All clear?" The Admiral shouted as the last of the sailors boarded the ship.

"All clear, sir." The sailor saluted him.

"Excellent." Greer smiled as he drooled over his cigar. He raised the binoculars to his eyes. His moment of ecstasy was close at hand. Greer gripped his binoculars with excitement. He and the crew members had stopped wearing goggles, saying it was like taking a shower with a raincoat on, or in more masculine company, having sex with a rubber. Saliva bathed the cigar stump that hung vulgarly from his mouth.

"On my order," Greer barked out. "Five, four, three, two..." He was trembling with anticipation.

"Admiral, WAIT!" The cry came from Second Officer Critner on the deck side.

Greer dropped the cigar from his mouth as he stared out into the ocean. "What in Sam Hell is that?"

"Sir, it looks like a woman," Critner reported.

"A WOMAN? Have you been out in the sun too long sailor?" Greer squinted into his binoculars. Sure enough, he could see a head of long blond hair bobbing up and down in the waves right off the shore.

"Goddamn woman messing up my life, well just don't stand there, fish her out!" Greer stormed off.

Corbin, Doc and Pots watched from the deck as the skiff returned. Pots stared at the boat as it bounced over the waves. "Damn if that woman doesn't look like...naw."

But Corbin had already pushed Pots aside and was

screaming at the top of his lungs, "Serena!" as he ran across the deck.

About two thousand crew members crowded around to see what one of the sailors was carrying in his arms. It was definitely Serena, wrapped in a blanket. Her long blonde hair was flowing out one end of the blanket and her legs, still joined together in a tail, hung out of the other end.

Greer stared at the unbelievable sight. "What in God's name is that?"

The man carrying Serena was in as much shock as the rest of the crew.

"We found her floating on the surface, sir." He looked at her peaceful face. " I think she's still alive."

Corbin pushed Greer aside and grabbed Serena's face in his hands.

"Serena!" He swept back her hair and kissed her forehead. Tears filled his eyes. He took her from the stunned sailor's arms.

"Do you know this...woman?" Greer said staring at his son-in-law in amazement.

Doc pushed his way through the opening. He opened Serena's eyes and looked at her pupils. "She's in shock. Let's get her down to sick bay."

Corbin pushed his way through the gawking crowd of sailors as he followed Doc to sick bay.

"Let them go," Greer told the sailors. "Send Corbin to my quarters when he's finished with the..." Greer waved his hands in the air. "Whatever she is!"

Serena was still unconscious while Corbin silently stood guard over her. He gently swept back a few wisps of her hair exposing a bruise on her forehead.

"Is she going to be okay, Doc?" Corbin asked anxiously.

"I hope so." Doc checked her pulse.

"What in the hell happened to her?" Corbin looked into Doc's eyes.

"Captain Corbin?" A sailor shouted. "Admiral Greer wants to see you topside."

"You go on. I'll take care of her." Doc smiled gently.

"Great, how am I going to explain this?" Corbin looked at Doc then walked off with the sailor.

Doc was taking good care of Serena when Corbin returned from his encounter with Admiral Greer. He'd sewn up some of her cuts and treated her abrasions. The swelling was going down but she hadn't regained consciousness. Because of this she still had her legs joined and Corbin and Doc had to request extra guards to keep the curiosity seekers away from sick bay.

Corbin pulled Doc aside. "What happened to her, Doc?"

Doc whispered over to Corbin, "I can't tell until I thoroughly examine her but..." Doc paused.

"What?" Corbin insisted.

"I think she's been raped, not just once but several times." Doc hated to tell Corbin the news.

Rage passed over Corbin's face. He slammed his fist against the steel wall.

"That goddamn...shark! I should have never left her. I'll kill him!" Corbin's face softened. "Is she going to be all right?"

"Physically, I think so. She'll need rest. Psychologically, I don't know. I don't know if she wants to wake up."

Corbin looked at her face as she slept. She looked like an angel, so sweet and peaceful. He stroked her chin as a tear rolled down his cheek.

"How could I have been so stupid to leave her?" Corbin choked back his tears.

Doc placed his arm on Corbin's shoulder. "You did what you had to do."

Serena was floating in the calm peaceful waters of her

home world with her mother by her side. Chaila smiled but her face turned into the face of a Shark. She lunged toward Serena. Serena swam away but the waters became dark and murky and Serena wasn't able to move, her arms and legs had become very heavy. She felt something tug at her foot and then she saw the water darken, this time with her own blood. She turned and noticed several sharks tearing off her limbs until all that remained was her head. Then Jaween appeared. He smiled, opened his great mouth and swallowed her head whole.

Serena awoke with a jolt. Beads of sweat covered her body. Corbin, who was lying in the bed beside her, reached his hand around her and gently stroked her hair and whispered into her ear.

"Shush, it's all right. Everything will be all right."

Serena tried to smile but felt the throbbing pain between her legs and the bruises on her body that reminded her of the most recent attack by Jaween's MerWarriors. She looked over at Corbin. He was so gentle and tender.

"Hungry?" He stroked her hair.

She gathered her will to live and nodded.

"Doc!" Corbin aroused the tireless physician.

"She up already?" Doc yawned as he checked Serena's vital signs, then looked over her bruises.

"And she's hungry!" Corbin beamed. "Well, let's hope Pots doesn't kill her with his cooking."

"That's good." Doc smiled.

"Doc says you've had quite an ordeal. Do you want to talk about it?" Corbin asked gently.

Serena shook her head no. Tears welled up in her eyes.

"My father is dead!" She lowered her head and cried softly. "Jaween killed him."

Corbin made a fist and tried to quiet his rage. He sat on the bed and took Serena in his arms and rocked her like a small child. "Don't worry, I'll never let anyone harm you again. I swear it."

Pots arrived with a tray of hot food. "Good to see you up again."

Doc took the plate from Pots and handed it to Serena. "I'd say eat this, it's good for you, but I have my reservations."

"I don't have to put up with this!" Pots acted hurt.

Serena picked up a piece of chicken with her fingers. "What kind of fish is this?"

"Chicken fish." Doc motioned for her to eat it.

Serena took a bite. "Mmm." She smiled then took another bite. "Good fish."

Pots smiled sarcastically at Corbin and Doc. "At least someone appreciates my cooking!"

The three men suddenly felt homesick. They had been so busy trying to leave MerWorld they had forgotten how happy they were there. They spent the rest of the day trying to cheer up Serena and reminiscing about the good old days. It was probably because of this they didn't notice what was happening right under their noses.

It was early morning, March 1, 1954, when a flash of blinding light illuminated the portholes inside the USS *Saratoga*. A raging fireball of intense heat that measured into the millions of degrees shot skyward at a rate of 300 miles an hour. Within minutes the monstrous cloud, filled with nuclear debris, shot up more than twenty miles and generated winds hundreds of miles per hour. These fiery gusts blasted the surrounding islands and stripped the branches and coconuts from the trees.

Doc, Pots, Corbin and Serena were rudely awakened by millions of tons of sand, coral, plants and sea life from Bikini's reef, and the surrounding lagoon waters, blasting into the air.

"Oh my God!" Corbin stared in shock as white ash fell like snow, covering the ship and its men.

"Don't go out there!" Doc hollered. "Batten down the

hatches, secure the windows!" Doc rushed around like a madman trying to seal off sick bay.

A powerful onslaught of tidal waves hit the ship, rocking her. Corbin stared out of the secured hatch as the tidal waves capsized the fleet of ships in front of them.

"Sweet Jesus, what have they done!" Pots cried out as if expecting an answer. The four of them just stood frozen taking in the horror of the moment.

One and a half hours after the explosion, twenty-three sailors who had watched in awe as a gritty white ash began to fall on them were in sick bay. Their skin began to itch and they were throwing up. One man died within the hour. On the nearby island where many of the islanders had been evacuated they did not understand what was happening. They observed with amazement as the radioactive dust fell two inches deep, turning their drinking water a brackish yellow. Children played in the fallout; when night fell their mothers watched in horror as their children began to experience severe vomiting and diarrhea. Mothers held their children in their arms to comfort them as huge chunks of hair fell into their hands. Both the island and the ships fell into a state of terrified panic. The people had received no explanations or warnings whatsoever from the United States government.

Inside sick bay Doc was dressing a wound on the back of a small native boy.

"Why doesn't this surprise me?" Corbin bathed the face of a sailor who was fried beet red.

John rushed in carrying the child with whom he had been playing the day before. "Doc, can you do something for him?"

Doc took the child from his arms.

"Sorry John, he's dead." Doc sighed and went over to ease the pain of a sailor who was vomiting.

Serena sat up. "Corbin." She reached out her hand and touched his face, then looked around the room. Tears filled her eyes. "How can Landers do this to one another?"

Corbin wiped her tears away. "I don't know." He kissed her forehead.

The next morning Admiral Greer was on the phone to the president. "Yes sir, we are very pleased. Overall it was a great success! Thank you sir, thank you."

The tremendous winds had died down and the waters were becalmed. Doc had lost twenty patients in the last twenty-four hours. The ones still alive were too weak to vomit and just lay in their beds praying for death, or were so burned they had mercifully passed out. Whatever the case, the room was as still as the ocean waters.

"Damn, I wish we could get a little breeze." Doc gazed out of the porthole. "That way the toxic fallout could disperse and become less lethal."

Corbin had fallen asleep holding Serena.

"Captain Corbin." A sailor looked at Serena. "I have orders to escort the...mermaid to the admiral."

The sailor walked toward Serena as if he were going to pick her up.

"I'll walk." Serena pulled her legs apart and sat up. The sailor froze.

Doc slapped the stunned sailor on the back. "Some pair of gams, eh!"

Serena discarded the sheet and strolled toward the door.

The sailor stared in shock at her beautiful body.

"Sacred vestments!" Corbin covered her with the sheet. "Now would be a good time for sacred vestments!" Corbin prodded the young sailor, "You look about her size."

The sailor looked at Corbin. "Yes sir!" He peeled off his clothes, then handed them to Corbin who quickly pulled the drapes around Serena.

By now several sailors had stuck their heads into sick bay. They were whistling wildly as more joined in the excitement.

Corbin helped Serena dress and escorted her through the sea of sailors.

Serena sat before Admiral Greer in his office. She was dressed in the oversized sailor's uniform that made her look like a little girl. But underneath was a woman and a great leader whose first concern was for her people.

"So you have legs?" Greer squinted as he looked at Serena's feet covered by the sailor's pants.

"Why did you do it?" Serena looked the Admiral straight in the eye. She had years of experience staring into Shark eyes.

"I like the feeling of power in the palm of my hand!" Greer pulled a piece of tobacco from his lips.

Serena smiled and looked deeper into his shark eyes. "You have no idea what power is."

A tenderness filled Serena's face and her body softened. She opened her mouth and it was as if she simply moved out of the way, willing a sound that was not her own to move through her body. It filled the whole room and quickly spread throughout the ship, then throughout the entire ocean.

Greer felt the hair on the back of his neck stand on end. His cigar hung from his gaping mouth as he was consumed by the most incredible sound he ever heard. It was beautiful, yet haunting, soothing, yet powerful. It possessed him and kept his body frozen and spellbound. He watched in wonder as the vibration spilled forth. Her voice carried power, not the raw destructive force he had unleashed the day before but a harmonized, intelligent force. It filled the ocean and the sky. The calm waters began to stir. The winds began to blow. The sea began to swell, bursting forth into waves that rose to a height of forty feet in a matter of seconds. The waves beat against the tiny ship, rocking it back and forth.

Greer came out of his trance. He reached out and grabbed his desk to steady himself. His cigar fell to the floor.

Alarms sounded. The crew sprang into alert.

A voice rang out on the intercom.

"Sir, it looks like some kind of typhoon just blew up out of nowhere! There are no reports of any weather in our area!"

Greer came to his senses. "Yeah, okay Winston, keep me posted."

Greer stood still staring at Serena's face.

The ship was fiercely rocking from side to side. Greer was doing all he could to stay on his feet. The winds whipped around the great ship, snatching up the poisonous ashes that still clung in the air and scattered them in her embrace.

"I want you to stop poisoning Mother Ocean!" Serena stared into the Admiral's eyes.

Greer shook with fear. "But my orders come from the president!"

"Then take me to him," Serena's voice commanded.

Greer held on for dear life. "Sure!"

CHAPTER TWENTY-TWO

"Needless to say, Greer was on the horn making arrangements with the White House. We arrived in San Francisco a few days later. For the first time in my life I really needed Corbin. It felt good. I dreaded leaving the ship. I was literally a fish out of water now and it was terrifying. I clung tightly to Corbin's strong body as he escorted me down the gangplank. Everyone had strict orders not to discuss a word about what was now known as Operation Fish Bait."

Serena hid her face in Corbin's shoulder as the Landers rushed about the dock screaming and hugging their loved ones. Corbin weaved in and out of them trying to find the car Greer had arranged to take them to their hotel as quickly as possible.

"What is this thing?" Serena squealed in Dolphin as Corbin helped her into the rear seat of the black limousine. The leather seats smelled of cigarette butts. Serena turned around and stared at the ocean as they drove away. The driver glanced in the rear view mirror at his strange passengers.

"I...I can open my window if the lady wants some ocean breeze?" The driver tried his best to manage the situation.

"That would be fine." Corbin squealed softly to Serena, "It's all right. You can see Mother Ocean from the hotel."

Serena squeezed Corbin's arm and calmed down as she felt the sea air in her lungs. She looked out the window at the ocean as it disappeared. Panic shook her body but she tried to calm herself.

"You promise?" Her voice was that of a small, scared child.

Greer had already informed the president of Serena's existence, but decided for the time being to withhold any information regarding her mystical origins and powers. He had changed his perspective and now saw Serena as an opportunity to further his military career. He protected her like his own private secret weapon. He had arranged for Serena to stay a few days at a hotel in San Francisco so she could get accustomed to living in the Lander environment. Then she would be flown in a private jet to Washington where Serena would meet with the president.

The bellman picked up Corbin's gunnysack with an air of arrogance. "And the lady's luggage?"

"She doesn't have any." Corbin held Serena's arm. She could barely walk.

The bellman opened the door to the suite and watched Corbin pick Serena up and carry her through the door. "Newlyweds?"

"Not exactly." Corbin laid Serena on the sofa.

"Oh, I see." The bellman crossed the room and opened the windows, exposing a balcony with a breathtaking view of the ocean. Serena sat up.

"Thank you." Corbin took the key. The bellman cleared his throat, obviously awaiting a tip.

"Is there anything else, sir, perhaps some ice?" He cleared his throat again and looked around the spacious room.

Corbin took his attention away from Serena. "Oh, uh, yes." He rummaged through his pockets and pulled out a gold coin. "Here, keep the change."

The bellman caught the coin, and without looking at it, he tucked it into his pocket then left the room shaking his head. "Cheapskate."

Corbin walked over to the phone and picked it up while Serena fidgeted with the balcony door, then walked out.

"Doc, uh, Doctor Taylor, please...Serena!" Corbin watched

as she stood on the balcony and took in a deep breath of sea air. "Uh, I don't know what room…what? Oh great, thank you."

All at once Serena looked down and squealed. Corbin dropped the phone and ran to her. Serena saw the ground beneath her, twenty-seven floors below. Her vision blurred, and a feeling of nausea rose in her throat.

Corbin's maternal instincts were being called upon and he realized he didn't have any. No wonder he had given up his son. He didn't know how to care for a baby, a woman, and certainly not a mermaid. He laid Serena on the sofa. Suddenly there was a knock at the door. Corbin opened it and much to his relief Doc strolled in.

"Thank God you're here! Where have you been?" Corbin was beside himself.

"I just wanted to make a few phone calls, you know, let a few people know I wasn't dead. Like the navy for one, I want to cash in on all that back pay!"

"I don't know what to do for her." Corbin scratched his head.

Doc checked Serena's vitals, then pulled out a couple of tablets. "Give her two of these and she should feel better by dinner."

He reached out and touched the rich burgundy fabric of the curtains and looked out over the bay of San Francisco. "Nice view. I'll check on her later, now I want see about that back pay!"

Corbin carried Serena into the bedroom. He propped Serena's head up and put the pills in her mouth, then gave her a sip of water. Exhausted, Corbin lay down on the bed beside Serena. He leaned his head against hers and fell into a deep sleep. By the time Corbin opened his eyes it was late afternoon. He looked around the room but Serena was gone.

"Holy shit!" Corbin rushed down to the lobby. He saw the bellman, who was studying his gold coin. "Excuse me."

The bellman's entire attitude toward Corbin had changed. "Yes, sir, how can I help you, sir?"

"Did you by any chance see the young lady I was with?"

"I believe she went to the swimming pool."

"The swimming pool? Oh no!"

"May I escort you, sir?"

"No, no thanks."

By the time Corbin reached the pool it was too late; Serena was swimming in the pool, the bottoms of her bathing suit were floating on the surface and she was singing and playfully splashing the water with her great tail.

She had modestly kept her bathing suit top on. On the far side of the pool a fat man in a Hawaiian shirt was madly snapping photos of her. He made a mad dash as soon as Corbin appeared.

"SERENA!" Corbin hollered.

Serena lifted her head out of the water. She quickly separated her legs and struggled to put the bathing suit bottoms back on.

"Serena! Are you crazy?" Corbin dragged her out of the water.

"I'm sorry Corbin, it's just that I felt so sick and no one was around so I..." She gently kissed his cheek. Corbin threw a towel over her head and hustled her toward the room.

"You're not angry?"

"Well..," Corbin knew how hard this was for her. He thought back to his first days in her world all those years ago and how she had helped him. "I'm glad you feel better but we can't take any more chances. Let's get you dry and then we should get you some decent clothes and maybe some dinner."

Back in the room Corbin dried her off like a shaggy dog. He looked down at her sweet innocent eyes. He had spent the past ten years wanting this woman, thinking about her day and night, and finally here they were alone, on dry land. But she looked so sweet and helpless he just couldn't take advantage of her, not after all she'd been through. What Serena needed most now was a friend, not a lover.

Corbin hugged her. "Get dressed, I'm taking you out on the town!"

Serena looked down at her bathing suit.

"Holy mother, what am I saying? Wait, I got it." Corbin picked up the phone, "Gift shop please. Just one minute. Hello, gift shop? Do you have something, I don't know, something really nice...elegant, that fits in all the right places."

The woman in the gift shop laughed. "I assume this is for a young lady? What is her size?"

Corbin looked at Serena dripping wet in her bathing suit. "Her size? Well...uh, she's got it in all the right places."

The woman could hear the lust in Corbin's voice. "I'll be right up."

Serena was decked out like a Christmas tree. She wore an elegant black dress with a lamb's wool sweater that itched her skin terribly. Corbin stood back, admiring his creation, while the woman from the gift shop sat on the floor beside piles of shoes, staring at Serena's oddly shaped feet.

"I'm afraid we just don't have anything in her size." The woman's face twisted. Corbin frowned. He picked up a pair of high heel shoes and cut an opening in the toes to give Serena more room. Then he looked at the heels.

"This will never work." He pulled a jack knife from his pocket and whacked off the heels. The sales woman screamed in protest, but Corbin just kneeled down like Prince Charming and slipped the shoe on Serena's foot.

Corbin stood up. "Baby, I think it's time for you to be introduced to San Francisco!"

Since Corbin had grown up in San Francisco he knew all of the right spots. Serena was feeling pretty good after her swim and the landsickness pills. She had a bit of a time walking at first but Corbin was very patient. He remembered trying to keep up with her in the plankton fields.

They grabbed a cable car at the top of the hill and rode it all the way down to Fisherman's Wharf. Serena held on and let the wind blow through her hair as she watched the brilliant sun setting over the ocean, bursting into a million shades of gold. She squealed as the trolley bell clanged and thought this was the most wonderful moment of her life.

Corbin took her to a local drugstore and threw Serena up on one of the stools. "Now this is something you have to try!"

The jukebox cranked out a new sound that Corbin was getting used to. It was called "Rock and Roll," and he liked it. The soda jerk leaned over the counter.

"Okay, Pops, what'll it be?"

"Uh..." Corbin smiled at Serena. "Two chocolate malts, extra chocolate. Hey, who's that singing?" Corbin motioned to the sound of a husky man's voice.

"Man where have you been? That's the King!" The young boy scooped up the ice cream and mixed in the chocolate.

"The King?" Corbin nodded. "Sounds kind of catchy."

Serena smiled and nodded as she sucked down her malt.

Corbin tossed the guy a gold coin and jerked Serena off the stool. "Come on, there's so much I want you to see!"

Serena followed Corbin as he led her through the fish market. She stared at the limp carnage.

"What's wrong?" Corbin noticed Serena was pinching her nose.

"Why are all these dead fish lying around! Why do the people touch them and look at them?" Serena squealed.

Corbin laughed. "They're going to buy them to take home and eat."

Serena's nose wrinkled. "But they are dead! And they smell."

A fishmonger and his wife stared at Serena like she had escaped from a mental hospital.

She was used to the MerWarriors ripping the heads from wriggling fish. "You Landers are so strange."

Corbin looked over at the couple and smiled, then pulled Serena out of the market. They continued to walk and came up to a bubblegum machine outside a store. Around the machine there was a group of teenagers buying gum. Corbin called to one of them.

"Hey, how would you like to trade two bubblegums for a gold coin?" Corbin handed the skinny thirteen-year-old with a crew cut the coin.

In shock, the teenager examined the coin and a big grin crossed his face. "For real?"

Corbin nodded.

"Thanks, Mister." The boy gave him the gumballs and ran off with his friends, clutching the coin in his hand.

Corbin turned to Serena. "Here's another one of our strange customs." He popped the gumball into her mouth. "Chew it, but don't swallow." Corbin popped the other gumball into his mouth.

Serena imitated Corbin's exaggerated chewing motion until he stuck his tongue through the wad and blew a bubble. Serena stared at him in amazement. "Just like the Whale Women. That's how they built MerWorld!"

Serena looked like an Oriental girl with hobbled feet respectfully walking behind her husband. Corbin slowed down his pace so she could catch up with him. The sun was gone and Serena felt the cool evening air against her skin and inhaled the fresh sea breeze as she watched the tiny colored lights of the city. There were so many strange sounds. Bells ringing, music blaring and Landers' voices laughing and talking. It was all so strange and mysterious to Serena.

Corbin took her to a little out of the way restaurant he knew in Chinatown. They sat on the rooftop, which was illuminated by the glow of brightly colored lanterns. Corbin ordered Peking duck and plum wine and by this time Serena was starting to feel a buzz.

"Serena, you've spent most of the evening looking up at the stars." Corbin reached out and captured her chin. She lowered her gaze from the sky and looked into his eyes.

"Can't I have just one glance?" He smiled.

"I'm sorry, Corbin, but I never had the chance to really see them. They're so...beautiful. I feel like I could reach out and touch one."

"They're light years away." Corbin was happy to have her attention again.

"How far is a...light year?" Serena stared into his eyes.

"Well, you know light travels faster than sound?" Corbin stumbled. He wished Doc was seated next to him, he'd be able to answer all her questions.

Serena thought a minute and answered slowly, "Yes."

"Well then a light year is the time it takes light to travel in a Lander year." Corbin was pleased with his answer. He thought it sounded rather scientific for a sailor.

"My, the universe is very big. In a way it is like one great ocean and we are all swimming in her."

Corbin smiled, "I guess you're right, all the planets, stars, moons and galaxies are just like living creatures floating around in their own orbit."

"Mother Universe." Serena moved her hand very slowly through the air in front of her.

"Serena, what are you doing?" Corbin looked around to see if anyone was looking.

"Yes, Yes I see." Serena smiled." I can feel it. It's not as strong as Mother Ocean's current but it is alive. It has a current of its own."

Corbin jumped in, "Consciousness."

Serena stumbled over the word as she rubbed her hands together forming a ball. She held the ball out in front of Corbin indicating for him to pass his hand through it. Corbin reluctantly obliged her.

"Can you feel it?"

Corbin looked around self-consciously. A couple next to them were staring at Serena.

"Serena!" Corbin motioned her to stop.

But Serena was mesmerized by the energy she was creating between her hands.

"It's like a bubble but you have to look harder or maybe..." She closed her eyes and blew air between her hands. "Softer." Then she took the ball of energy and pushed it into Corbin's face.

He felt a warm flush of heat and his demeanor melted as a wave of love spread throughout his body. He found the entire experience profoundly energizing and arousing. The wave passed from his head down to his toes.

"Serena!" Corbin cried out, "Stop that!"

Serena smiled then returned her gaze to the stars.

The couple close to them had noticed Serena's strange actions. They whispered to one another and looked at Serena and Corbin.

"I wonder if I can..." Serena opened her mouth and softly let out a beautiful sound. A light breeze blew across the veranda where they were seated. Her voice sang louder and the breeze picked up, rustling the leaves and clicking the china.

"That's enough, Serena," Corbin whispered out the side of his mouth as he watched the couple and the waiter looking around, but the winds picked up. A wine glass fell from a table and broke, napkins blew across the room. But Serena was moved by the melody and kept singing the enchanting song.

"Serena. Stop it!" Corbin whispered louder.

The winds whipped through the rooftop. A man's hairpiece blew off and a woman's scarf covered her face. The waiter's tray landed on top of them and the china dropped to the floor breaking into a thousand pieces. The waiter shouted frantically in Chinese.

Serena opened her eyes.

"Let's get out of here!" Corbin laid a few gold coins on the table and grabbed Serena's arm, pulling her through the mini tornado she had created. They spilled out on the street laughing as they left the ravaged restaurant behind them.

It had been a wonderful evening. Serena was feeling tipsy from the plum wine. She had been walking on her feet all day and they weren't used to such abuse. Corbin kicked open the door of their elegant suite carrying Serena in his arms. He tripped as he approached the bed and fell on top of her. She giggled as Corbin pulled himself off her chest laughing.

"I guess I won't be going back there for a while!" Corbin stumbled over his words. He was also feeling a buzz.

Serena giggled. Corbin stopped laughing and kissed Serena tenderly. "I love you Serena!"

Fear darted across Serena's face. Corbin kissed her very gently. She felt the longing in her body and tried to relax. Corbin teased her with his moist lips, then traced his tongue around her mouth. Whether it was the plum wine or the gentleness of his kiss, Serena felt her body doing something she never thought possible: relaxing under the hand of a man. Corbin moved his lips to her neck and slowly down to her breasts. He sweetly cupped her bosom and licked her nipples, then reached his hands down to her breasts and circled around her navel with his fingertips and finally to the magical space between her thighs. Serena tensed up as Corbin's hands brushed across the tiny suckers between her legs. He did his best not to let them get in his way as he touched her in that special place. The deep, constant massaging mixed with his gentle kisses caused Serena's body to instinctively vibrate with the rhythmic movements of his hand. She was opening herself to him: her body, her heart and finally her soul. She suddenly felt a flash of fear as pleasure swelled in her groin.

Corbin moved his mouth to her ear and whispered, "Relax," as his tongue danced around her earlobe.

She felt her body relax further as a shudder of pleasure ran through her. She clutched him tightly and her body buckled and shook. Frightened by the power of the climax that ran through her, tears welled up in her eyes and she lost all control, giving into her pleasure as Corbin intensified his movements to bring her to an even higher climax. Tears bathed her face. "I love you," she gasped.

Corbin delicately kissed her as his muscular body trembled and slipped inside her. His movements were slow, gentle and so tender that tears spilt from her already moist eyes.

"It's okay, baby," Corbin whispered as his rhythmic movements sent waves of pleasure undulating through her. It was so different from the horrible experience she'd had with Jaween and his MerWarriors and Corbin did his best to help her know the difference.

She lay back as if asking for more. His body melded into hers. There was no division, no distinction between them. He was no longer a Lander and she was no longer a Mermaid. Their bodies were joined together and it was impossible to tell where one began and the other ended. They were one... MerLander. The rhythms of their bodies increased until they both climaxed together. They held each other tightly and drifted off into a deep slumber.

During a dream Serena saw herself floating in the Abyss, before the Portal of Time. She stared at the brilliant white light, mesmerized by its beauty, power and brilliance. As she stared into it she saw the face of the dark MerWarrior who had taken her mother's body from her. He was strikingly handsome. His face was chiseled yet rugged. He had long jet black hair that hung past his shoulders. His brilliant blue eyes gazed at her from the other world. They had an iridescent glow.

"Serena, I am your father Triton. It is true the blood of the Shark courses through your veins. But this is nothing for you to fear. You must not believe the falsehoods spread about me or my father Poseidon. These were spread by Sharfina and before her by my own mother Sharkara. Your mother and I were bound together in love and out of that love sprang you. You are the balance between the best of the Shark and the Whale. Without this balance all will be lost!"

The whale shark! Serena thought as she gazed on at the most handsome of all Mer Warriors. *"My father? Why have I been robbed of knowing you?"*

Serena held her hand out toward the image on the other side of the Portal. She felt her fingers touching his. His hand opened and grasped hers, and then in one quick movement she found herself on the other side.

"Here, there is no time." Triton wrapped his mighty arms around her. She felt so much love enfolding her that it was as if her heart would break.

"Father." Serena felt all the lost years fulfilled in that one magnificent embrace.

"There are no more boundaries, no limits now that you have awakened. But you must return to your world and let the Shark inside you guide you through the treacherous times ahead."

Triton's face vanished and Serena opened her eyes. She felt wonderful. The lovemaking session had energized, healed and restored her and the visit with her father had awakened something dormant within her. She snuggled next to Corbin. It felt so different than the horrible experience which had left her half dead and sick in her soul.

How strange, she thought, as she watched the sunlight dance through the burgundy drapes and felt Corbin's strong powerful arms around her, *the same act can destroy or rejuvenate someone depending on the intent.*

Corbin propped himself up on his elbow. "I don't know about you but I'm starving."

Serena felt a rumbling in her stomach as well. The late night sex session had stirred her appetite.

"Leave it to me." Corbin rolled over and picked up the phone, exposing his perfectly shaped rear end. Serena giggled and ran her fingers lightly over one of his cheeks tickling him.

"Stop it! Hello, room service." Corbin blushed slightly and motioned for her to curtail her playful Dolphin tactics.

"Yes, this is room three-o-four and we'd like breakfast...

well, do you have any eggs Benedict, good, good. Can you make it with poached salmon?"

"What are eggs Benedict?" Serena interrupted.

Corbin signaled for her to be quiet. "And bring plenty of bacon, oh and fresh milk, and French toast soaked in maple syrup and butter. Yes, and coffee, don't forget the coffee, a big black pot of it, and fruit! All the fresh fruit you can find!" Corbin put his hand over the receiver, "Finally a decent cup of coffee."

"Coffee?" Serena stood up exposing her exquisitely naked body. She walked over to the large burgundy drapes and pulled them apart, illuminating the room with the morning sunshine. She was awed by the sunrise. The brilliant reds, oranges and golds flooded into the room silhouetting Serena's shapely ass.

Corbin felt himself becoming aroused and suddenly the food wasn't his most dominant craving. "Could you give us about half an hour before you deliver that?"

Serena turned around. She was beaming. Her entire body caught the glow of the morning sun as it reflected through her golden hair and draped over her ripe full breasts.

"Uh, better make that an hour, thanks." Corbin fumbled to put the phone in its cradle.

"Come here, you little siren." He threw the covers back exposing his excitement.

"Again?" Serena walked toward him. He leaned forward and kissed her breasts. This time the siren was less inhibited. She knew what she wanted. She pushed Corbin back on the bed and slowly climbed on top of him. Corbin looked up at her with a sense of surprise and perhaps a little fear.

"Serena, take it easy." He was pinned under her; he knew he could easily push her off but he was amazed by the transformation. *Was this the same inhibited mermaid he so carefully seduced the night before?*

Serena felt something stir inside her. It was the Shark in her now surfacing. She was no longer the frightened, victimized MerMaiden Jaween's MerWarriors had ravaged.

She was overcome with desire. She wanted to be in charge, to dominate, to aggressively go after what she wanted, and she wanted Corbin. She too had the blood of the Shark inside her. Serena placed her tongue in Corbin's ear, then bit down on his earlobe. Corbin cried out in pain.

"Easy, easy. I promise you'll be satisfied." Corbin smiled gently. She now knew the pleasure of lovemaking and was greedy for it. She smiled and kissed Corbin deeply, then straddled him, grabbing hold of his throbbing member and putting him inside her.

"Serena, wait, I..." Corbin was both excited by her hunger and a bit intimidated. He tried to pull back but his body betrayed him. She moved her hips back and forth, vigorously riding him like a great sperm whale.

"Serena...wait, God that feels so..." Corbin was overcome by the power he felt coursing through her body. It was as if all the currents of the Ocean ran though her and into him. With each gyration Serena seemed to become more and more energized. It was as if she was receiving life force from him, but it wasn't draining him, instead it was electrifying, intense and powerful beyond anything he'd ever experienced. All at once, when he could take no more, they both exploded into one another. She collapsed into Corbin's arms as he wrestled to breathe. He felt as if he was dying.

Serena lay back. A great wave flushed through her body and into her face creating a haloed effect around her. Corbin was able to take a few deep breaths. He looked into her eyes and panted out a few words.

"What... just...happened?" Corbin stared at her.

Serena smiled, "MerLove."

There was a knock at the door.

"Room service!" the waiter shouted.

Could it have been a whole hour? Corbin was amazed as he watched Serena jump up from the bed; he thought she would take off, flying across the room, with all the energy she exuded.

He tried to raise his body but it collapsed back into the bed. He felt as if a truck had hit him.

"It's even better underwater." Serena skipped to the door.

"How do you know?" Corbin was still panting.

She turned around smiling. "It lasts for three days."

"Hey, put some clothes on!" Corbin yelled as he managed to sit up.

Serena had her hand on the door. "Oh yes, I almost forgot." She picked up a thin silk robe and threw it on.

"More than that!" Corbin protested but found himself back flat on the bed.

"Jesus!" He cried in vain.

"Here you go Ma'am," It was the bellman from before. He rolled the table into the room and just about crashed into the wall when he got a load of Serena's flimsy frock. Corbin managed to sit up and cover himself with a sheet but that was the extent of his range of motion.

"Your, your...poached salmon Benedict." The bellman raised the top of the dish, exposing the lavish spread, all the while keeping his eyes on Serena's body through the transparent robe.

Serena smiled and squealed in Dolphin, "Oh look Corbin!"

The bellman gave a side glance at Corbin, wishing he would be absorbed into the wallpaper.

Corbin was trying to find the strength to stand.

"Your French toast." The bellman was getting more and more excited as Serena jumped and ran around the table, taking the lids off the dishes and smelling them.

"THAT WILL BE ALL THANK YOU!" Corbin blurted out as he tripped over his bed sheet.

"Are you all right sir?" The bellman rushed over.

"Quite!" Corbin awkwardly held the sheet in one hand and signed the tab with the other." That will be all!" Corbin smiled.

The bellman rushed to the door, and then turned around, "Oh I almost forgot your newspaper, sir."

"Just GET OUT!" Corbin screamed.

The bellman laid the paper on the table and scurried out of the room.

"Corbin, what's wrong with you?" Serena rushed over to help him up.

"What's wrong with me? Serena, look at what you're wearing! It's not decent!" Corbin's eyes fell upon Serena's face on the front page of the San Francisco *Daily News*.

"Decent?" Serena stuck her finger into the maple syrup. "Mmm, delicious!"

Corbin grabbed the paper as the phone rang. He studied the newspaper's headline that read: "Mermaid in San Francisco." There was a picture of Serena splashing about in the hotel pool with her mermaid tail for all the world to see.

Just then the phone rang and Corbin picked it up.

"Yes sir. I saw it, Admiral." Corbin looked at Serena who, like a child, was licking her sticky fingers full of maple syrup.

"What do you suggest we do?" Corbin sighed, "All right. I'll have her ready, sir."

"This is very good." Serena was still playing with the syrup jar. "Aren't you hungry?"

"I was." Corbin held up the paper and frowned at Serena, who dropped her head.

"I'm sorry." Serena sulked.

Corbin picked up the phone, "Doctor Taylor."

"Corbin, are you angry with me?"

"Doc, did you get a gander at this morning's news? Yeah, well, so much for keeping her under wraps. Greer wants us to leave for Washington on the double. He says the press is all over the main lobby. We'll have to make a run for it out the back. He's got a plane waiting for us at the base. Yeah, well,

I want you there for Serena. Pots is with his family. Yeah, it's better for him if he stays out of this, it could get messy...okay." Corbin hung up the phone and started to dress.

Serena snuggled against him. "Forgive me?"

Corbin melted. "How can I be mad at you?" He kissed her on the forehead. "Come on, get some clothes on."

CHAPTER TWENTY-THREE

"The publicity caused quite a stir. The president had been sent a copy and was anxious to meet me. As you can imagine, Greer did his best to keep his secret weapon secret, but I was now on the front page of every major newspaper in the world. It had become a matter of national security with both the government and the navy's finest working to keep Operation Fish Bait under wraps.

The plane ride from San Francisco was rough but I did my best to cope. I was just getting over my landsickness when I was hit with airsickness. The hardness part was the dryness. I did my best to keep my legs moist but it was becoming increasingly more difficult.

A swarm of reporters gathered outside the White House as I was secretly escorted into the compound through an underground tunnel. I held onto Corbin's muscular arm for support as I walked into the crisp elegance of the Oval Office. The president stood up to meet me, his eyes fixated on my large feet. He tried his best to ignore them, smiling politely, but he didn't have that kind of concentration. His balding head was covered with a few well-meant strands of hair, and his gray suit was neatly pressed. He forced a smile and extended his hand toward me. I smiled, took his hand, and opened my mouth to speak, but instead of words gushing forth that familiar feeling of nausea arose in my throat and I baptized the president's pants with vomit. A swarm of Secret Service men sprang from every nook and cranny, creating a human shield between the president and me."

"Sorry sir, she has landsickness, compounded with airsickness," Corbin offered, helping Serena to the sofa while one of the Secret Service men pawed at the president's crotch with a wet cloth.

"Could I have a glass of water and a damp towel, please?" Doc was examining Serena as he groped for another landsick pill. He mopped and patted down her forehead with the cool water.

Corbin knelt beside her and whispered gently in her ear, "I guess you're not much of a flyer, good thing I'm not in the air force."

Doc handed him the towel and he wiped down her face. The president, who was still in a daze, came to his senses. He pushed the Secret Service men away from his crotch and bellowed out, "Greer, what is the meaning of this? This woman is ill!"

"I'm sorry sir, but..." Greer was interrupted.

"I'm all right." Serena, remembering the urgency of her visit, gathered her strength and sat up. "I asked to speak with you on behalf of my people." Serena stood up emitting strength and dignity. In just a few short moments she had changed from a frail seasick young girl to a powerful leader. The president noted the change and stood silent.

"I am Serena, Queen of MerWorld," Serena announced.

"Won't you sit down?" The president indicated the sofa she had just risen from and then took a seat across from her. He shot a sideways glance at Greer. The president was impressed by her courage, fortitude and dedication. He poured on his politician charm.He could see now she was more than a weak female but had the potential of becoming a formidable enemy.

"No thank you, sir." Serena turned her back to the men and focused on her story. "Many seasons ago our people lived together in harmony. We traded with Landers who traveled on ships through our waters."

The president's eyebrows raised and he whispered to Greer, "Their waters?"

Greer made a gesture indicating the president should dismiss Serena's politically incorrect statement and listen.

Serena turned around to gain his full attention. She stared boldly into his eyes. "We respected each other's differences and uniqueness. But when your people took to the seas by the hundreds and began the merciless slaughter of our sacred whales, the citizens of Mer were forced to see your kind as hostile. We burrowed ourselves deep within the ocean floor, taking refuge in great underwater caverns. We took great precautions to hide from you and soon you forgot all about us. Only a lone fisherman or a shipwrecked sailor would catch a glimpse of us from time to time. We were glad to be forgotten by you. But we can hide from you no longer. Now you are poisoning our waters, destroying our cities, and killing our children!" Serena's eyes became moist and her voice soft.

"Cities?" The president turned to Greer in shock.

"We have nowhere else to hide. I have come here to ask you to stop the destructive bombardment of our home waters and leave us in peace!"

The president whispered in Greer's ear, "Is she for real?"

Greer whispered back, "Just play along."

"Damn it Nathan!"

Corbin stepped forward. "If I may, sir..."

"And who in blue blazes are you?" The president eyed Corbin up and down.

"Captain James Corbin, U.S. Navy, sir. My sub went down ten years ago during the war and I and my associate, Dr. Taylor," Corbin pointed at Doc who smiled and made a two finger salute, "have spent the past ten years living among these MerPeople."

"How in the hell did you do that?" The president shouted.

"Bubbles, sir." Doc cut in.

"Bubbles? MerPeople? You expect me to believe all this?" The president looked at Greer.

"I'm afraid so, sir." Corbin stared into the president's eyes. The president shook his head with disgust then turned to Greer who motioned him toward Serena.

He stood up and took her hand. "I apologize. I had no idea."

He looked at Serena in amazement and stared at her legs, then whispered to Corbin. "Aren't they supposed to...you know."

Corbin jumped in, "In the water, sir."

"Oh well," the president coughed and glared over at Greer, "I will take your petition under consideration when I meet with my advisors."

Greer smiled and nodded in approval.

"Until which time I would like you and...your...friends to be my guests tonight at a reception we are having here at the White House. Please accept my personal invitation."

"Thank you." Serena bowed and took Corbin's arm as he escorted her out of the Oval Office. Greer stayed behind while Doc, Corbin and Serena were escorted to their hotel.

It was an elegant hotel in downtown Washington, tastefully ornate with the right balance between old world politics and new world capitalism. Serena, Corbin and Doc stepped into the enormous suite decorated with elaborately framed mirrors, costly brass fixtures, marble floors, and three huge bedrooms, each with their private bath. Sprawling arched columns were interwoven among the marvels of modern technology. A large color TV was positioned between lavish gold curtains in front of a floral wallpaper which conjured up images of Betsy Ross's bedroom, while the bathrooms were a potpourri of colored tiles and Italian marble.

"Do you think they are trying to buy us?" Corbin said as he stared at the crown molding on the ceiling.

"Naw!" Doc wandered into his room, threw down his duffle bag, and kicked back on the oversized bed.

Serena headed straight for the bathroom, which was larger than most bedrooms. Inside was an enormous oval tub fashioned out of pink Italian marble with a large brass water faucet in the shape of a fish, which spouted water from its mouth. Serena filled the bath and poured a box of sea salt into the water. She undid the fasteners on her dress, heaved a great sigh, and slid into the opulent elegance of her bathtub. Her thigh suckers instinctively joined together and her tail flapped against the smooth marble surface. She submerged into the peace and quiet, inhaling the salt water into her lungs. Her head pounded from all the busy, senseless chatter of the Lander World. Since her arrival there were always loud sounds about her, bells clanging, Lander voices squawking, car engines humming, horns honking. Her soul longed for the inner silence only water could afford.

"Serena, Serena!" Corbin's pounding shook the room.

"Come out of there! You've been in there for three hours!"

Serena squealed something unpleasant to him in Dolphin.

"Come on, we've got to get something for you to wear for tonight!"

Serena pulled her head out of the water. "But I have sacred vestments!" Serena squealed and submerged herself again.

Corbin and Doc and an entourage of Secret Service men spent the afternoon in Georgetown going from one posh boutique to another. Corbin didn't know much about shopping, but he did know what looked good on Serena.

The sales clerk stared at Serena's large, oddly shaped webbed feet as she struggled with yet another suffocating dress.

"My goodness," Serena said as she pulled her head out from under the mounds of fabric. "You certainly take your sacred vestments very seriously, and you have so many, one for every occasion!"

The sales clerk winked at her. "We do indeed honey, after this I'll take you upstairs to lingerie."

Seven dresses later Serena finally found her fit. She stood in front of the mirror squealing with delight. Corbin snuck up behind her with his eyes lit up by her dazzling beauty. He whispered in her ear, "You look magnificent."

Serena beamed. "What kind of seaweed is this?"

"Uh, silk sea...weed." The woman made a face. "And it is five hundred bucks."

It was a beautiful, low cut, emerald green mermaid dress. It showed off Serena's generous cleavage, embraced her small waist and accentuated her ample hips, then fanned out at her knees, covering her feet completely. Serena loved it.

One of the customers inched her way closer to Serena. Her face and fins had become a prize paparazzi piece posted on the cover of every tabloid from Bangor, Maine to Chula Vista, California.

"Look! There's the mermaid!" the woman cried out, pointing to Serena. A group of shoppers crowded around. The Secret Service men surrounded her while Corbin and Doc whisked her out the back door and into the limousine.

The baffled saleswoman ran after them. "Wait! What about the bill?"

Doc shouted, "Send it to the White House!"

"I had been so busy coping with my new environment I didn't realize what a sensation I had become. Overnight I'd become an international celebrity. Corbin was beginning to see how this could become useful, not only in helping the MerPeople, but also in insuring my safety. He decided to wait for the appropriate opportunity to take advantage of it."

Greer was seated in his steam room with a glass of forty-year-old brandy. A cigar hung from his mouth while he opened the evening paper. Serena's picture once again filled the front page. "Mermaid in Washington..." the headlines glared at him. Greer flung his brandy snifter on the tile floor. "Goddamn siren!"

Except for the publicity, everything was transpiring just as he had planned. He was in control of the most powerful secret weapon since the hydrogen bomb: a woman who could control the oceans. Heaven knows what other powers she possessed, not to mention the other inhabitants of that underwater world of hers. Imagine, a secret underwater army only he could control!

He'd learned the art of instilling trust to break down the enemy's defenses, and then at the precise moment when they were most vulnerable, he'd take control. But now with all this publicity Serena could achieve favor in the public eye. She could find herself with a powerful ally, no longer the defenseless mermaid in a hostile environment at his mercy. Greer knew the language of politics. But the public was always a wild card.

The White House was ablaze. Ambassadors, dignitaries and royalty from all parts of the globe lined the walls as Serena, the unofficial representative of MerWorld, strolled into the room with Corbin and Doc on either arm. A quiet murmur spread throughout the crowd as if Cinderella had entered the prince's ball. Couples stared and whispered as they swept gracefully across the floor in time with the music from an elaborate orchestra positioned on a platform at the far end of the great ballroom. Serena felt her heart skip a beat.

"It's so beautiful!" Serena whispered to Corbin as she clung tightly to his arm.

"Hold your head up, Your Majesty." Corbin whispered.

Serena felt her spine straighten.

"As far as I'm concerned Serena's the only real royalty here." Doc spoke loudly to Corbin as they walked past the upturned noses of European kings and queens.

Waiters in white suits carried trays filled with lobster canapés, Russian caviar and French champagne. They passed among the elegantly clad men and women.

Corbin reached out and grabbed a flute of champagne. "Peasants!"

He led Serena straight toward the president catching him slightly off guard. "Mr. President."

The president turned abruptly and choked on a piece of caviar he had just stuffed into his mouth.

"So good of you to come." The president reached out his arm and grabbed the first lady, "Darling this is...a...a..."

"Queen Serena," Corbin interjected, slightly annoyed.

"Queen?" The first lady peered down at Serena. She noticed one of her odd shaped feet protruding from under her dress. "And where are you from, Serena?"

Greer quickly interrupted. "One of the islands in the North Pacific." Greer pulled Corbin to the side. "Good God man, can't you keep your woman under control? I thought we agreed it was best to keep a low profile!" Greer clenched his cigar.

"Best for whom, Admiral?" Corbin smiled.

"And how long are you staying with us, my dear?" The first lady looked like she was making a great effort to be polite.

"Until your husband stops murdering my people." Serena smiled and took one of the pretty fluted glasses of champagne while the president went into a coughing convulsion.

"Excuse me, Captain Corbin?" An attractive woman with heavy eye makeup and a beehive hairdo tapped Corbin on the shoulder. "I'm Cynthia Brinkle. I'm with NBC. I know you're not officially permitted to discuss why Serena is visiting our country but word has it that it has something to do with the atomic testing being conducted in the Pacific?"

Corbin stared at Greer who was patting the president on the back. He took a deep swig, and moved her away from the shark-infested waters. "Keep talking."

"If you were to, say...bring Serena around to our studio tomorrow morning at around seven o'clock, I can promise she would find a very sympathetic audience." Miss Brinkle smiled and batted her eyelashes doused in mascara.

"Sympathetic you say?" Corbin cocked his ears. He knew better than to trust a reporter, or anyone associated with the press, for that matter, but he did feel the need to ally himself with someone other than Greer and the half dozen politicians he had lining his pocket. "How's that?"

"Well, quite frankly we've been searching for some kind of platform to oppose the atomic testing and, well...if Serena is what I think she is...we'd have a sensational vehicle to grab public awareness."

"Sensational huh? Is that what you're looking for, Miss Brinkle, sensation?" Corbin turned and watched Greer whispering into the president's ear. It was time for Corbin to make his move. He was not a political man but they were now on dry land, his turf. He watched Serena as she interacted with the elite. She held herself so regally anyone would know she was royalty, no matter what part of the globe she inhabited. It was high time MerWorld was recognized for what it was: a nation that simply happened to lie beneath the ocean. Corbin looked back into the eyes of this woman. They were trying their best to charm him, but underneath the mascara and pounds of foundation he could see Shark eyes.

"We'd be delighted." Corbin smiled the same phony smile right back at her.

"We'll see you at seven then?" Cynthia oiled forth her hand.

Corbin nodded and shook the clammy member.

Doc, who was observing the scene from afar, quickly pulled himself away from a similar conversation and rallied beside Corbin.

"You know, it's funny." Doc picked up a glass of champagne from a passing waiter. "I kinda miss MerWorld."

"Really?" Corbin nodded.

Doc grinned. "At least down there you knew when you were face to face with a Shark."

"Yeah." Corbin shook his head and looked over at Serena, noticing she was surrounded by top brass.

"Looks like Serena has been surrounded, I'd better execute a retreat." Corbin slipped over and whispered something to the leader of the orchestra.

Stranger on the Shore, that sexy sax number that Corbin had first seduced Serena with all those years ago in the *Poseidon* filled the ballroom. Serena looked up, her eyes peered beyond the sea of generals' faces and searched the room for her Corbin. Corbin surprised her from behind.

"I hate to steal her away from you gentlemen, but I believe this is our dance." Corbin grabbed Serena by the waist and smugly pulled her into him.

"Oh Corbin, I can't perform your Lander ritual in front of everyone!"

"Just relax and pretend we're back inside my big fish." Corbin ran his lips along her cheeks. Serena clung tight to him. Soon she felt her body relax. Corbin held her close and whispered in her ear.

"That's it baby, just relax, and hold onto me. I've got you." Corbin laid his cheek against hers and closed his eyes. Soon the room, the sea of faces all disappeared into a blur. Serena was fathoms away under the sea in the belly of the great beast that had brought Corbin to her. Their bodies melded together.

"Pretty good for a mermaid." One of the generals laughed.

"If it's true, what kind of army do you think they have down there?" Admiral Pruett asked Greer.

"No comment, gentlemen." Greer smiled smugly at the old military hounds and walked away.

"If that asshole thinks he's going to keep this whole sweet thing all to himself he's got another thing coming," Admiral Pruett grunted, and the others nodded in agreement.

Corbin held Serena tightly and whispered into her ear, "Maybe after we get MerWorld squared away you could settle up here with me. It's not so bad, this Lander World of mine, is it?"

Corbin was trying to convince himself as much as Serena when a tap on the shoulder interrupted him. It was the president cutting in.

"Excuse me Captain, but it seems like your little mermaid and I got off on the wrong foot." The president bowed and extended his arm. "May I have a chance to redeem myself?"

Corbin looked down at his foot edging next to Serena's. "Are you sure that's the right one?" He hesitantly handed Serena over to him.

The president laughed nervously and took Serena in his arms. "My, you look lovely this evening!"

"Thank you." Serena looked deep into his eyes sizing him up once and for all.

The president stared down into Serena's ample cleavage.

"Have you had a chance to commune with the Great Ones?"

"Commune?" The president looked into Serena's lovely face.

"Yes, you said you needed to have time to..."

"Oh that, yes of course, no not yet. But I promise to call them into my office first thing tomorrow. My you are a pretty little thing." The president whirled her around.

Serena felt nauseous.

"How could Mother Ocean or the Great Whale Mother possibly fit inside your tiny office?" Serena laughed. "Or the wisdom of the Ancient Ones?" Serena looked into his eyes.

"Beg your pardon?"

"I'm sorry, perhaps you Landers consult with...who will you be consulting with?"

The president was looking down Serena's dress and enjoying the view as he spoke. "What, sweetheart? Oh, my advisors, why there they are right over there." The president pointed to the group of generals and admirals Serena had just escaped from.

"*Sharks!*" Serena thought as she felt her Shark blood boiling inside her veins. She stopped dancing and stared into the president's eyes. How could she have not noticed? She had been thrown off because they were on land, but there she was staring into the eyes of a Shark, a Shark wearing Dolphin skin, pretending to laugh and dance, but all the while stalking her like prey.

"Oh no, there goes our girl." Doc nudged Corbin and they stared at the president and Serena in the middle of the dance floor. They watched Serena as she stood still staring at the president. Everyone else's gaze turned toward the couple.

"Oh man, I hope she doesn't punch him!" Corbin whispered.

Serena could hear her father's words. *You will need your Shark instinct in the times that lie ahead. No longer will I be the innocent victim, fed upon by ravenous Sharks! I too have Shark in me. But like the Whale Shark, I can tame those characteristics and bring them to their highest qualities.* Serena's thoughts focused.

"Your Majesty, are you all right?" the president had been repeating that question several times. Serena's face was flushed and red. Her thoughts came back to the dance floor and to the president who stood in front of her.

"I'm...wonderful!" She tossed her head back and let loose a loud laugh, then grabbed firmly hold of the president's arm and began to lead. She whirled him around the floor and the president felt his dinner rising in his stomach. Before he could stop, Serena grabbed hold of the president's saggy rear end and squeezed hard.

A wave of shock passed through the guests while the president's face flushed red as he felt his buttocks being groped by a mermaid.

The first lady dropped her flute of champagne on the marble floor. Serena smiled, released him and walked over to Corbin and Doc.

"Cinderella, I think the clock is striking midnight." Corbin smiled at Serena.

"Shall we?" Doc and Corbin both extended their arms and Serena took a hold of them. "That's no Lander, that's a Shark," Serena said indignantly as she looked back over her shoulder at the president who was apologetically explaining something to the first lady.

Doc and Corbin looked at each other.

"You know Corbin, I couldn't agree with you more!" And the three marched out the door.

CHAPTER TWENTY-FOUR

The next morning Corbin took Serena to the TV studio. She squirmed and squealed in Dolphin as the makeup people struggled to powder and paint her face. Serena pushed aside a large powder puff as she clicked and squealed in Dolphin. Corbin clicked and squealed back.

"I'm not thrilled about this either, Serena, but after seeing what we're up against last night I think a little public awareness of MerWorld is our only hope." Corbin conveyed in Dolphin. The makeup crew stared at Corbin as he uttered the strange sounds. Serena clicked back loudly. Miss Brinkle rushed over.

"What did she say?" Her face was aghast, never had she heard such strange sounds. She stared down at Serena's feet and tried her best not to stare but her eyes kept wandering back to them.

"Uh, you don't want to know, but I would advise you to have your people stop putting that stuff on her face, she doesn't like it."

"But we have to put on some pancake. You see we can't have any glare..." Miss Brinkle nodded to the makeup man.

The makeup man pushed a large powder puff into Serena's face while a hairdresser plastered hairspray on her golden tresses. Powder and hairspray were flying everywhere and Serena could barely breathe. She took a large breath as a hand with bright red lipstick seized the moment to paint her mouth. Serena could stand it no more. She opened her mouth and let out a long, shrill squeal that caused everyone to cover their ears. The set walls shook and one of the cameras fell over. The rest of the technical equipment trembled. The entire TV crew doubled over in pain. They felt as if their eardrums would burst. Underwater, Serena's voice had been devastating enough, but without the protective buffer of the water her voice had become a lethal weapon.

When Serena saw the terrible devastation her sounds were causing she quickly stopped. The entire TV crew was on its knees. They looked up and slowly began to rise. A huge light fell to the floor, nearly striking the makeup man who frantically threw some of his makeup tools into a box and scurried away. Miss Brinkley adjusted her hairpiece, which had fallen to the side, and cleared her throat.

"Well, uh, perhaps she has enough makeup. In fact, she looks just fine. Shall we?" Miss Brinkle pointed her hand toward the set.

The crew was propping the set back up, someone was sweeping up broken glass and the whole place looked like a bomb had exploded.

"We've got five minutes to air!" a nervous little man screamed out. Miss Brinkle tried to pull herself together. She sat in her chair and indicated for Serena and Corbin to take a seat in the two chairs beside her. She looked at the camera, assuming her *on the air pose*. Her wiglet was still slightly off. The cameraman was about to say something when he noticed his lens was cracked.

The entire crew scurried about looking for another lens while one of the team members chimed out, "One minute to air."

"Oh God!" The director panicked as the cameraman unscrewed the lens, fumbling and dropping the new one. The entire room was on pins and needles as the countdown continued. Serena cast a mischievous smile toward Corbin who quickly shot her back a parental scowl.

The cameraman slipped on the new lens and triumphantly screamed, "Got it!" just as the countdown came to a halt and the director called out, "Action."

Cynthia Brinkle was caught off guard. She struggled to adjust herself and stuttered for a moment. "Uh, uh Good morning, this is an NBC live broadcast coming to you from our nation's capital where today we have a very special guest with us."

The makeup man was trying to signal to Cynthia that her wiglet was still on wrong by making charade like movements.

"We would like to welcome our guests Serena and Captain Corbin of the U.S. Navy." Cynthia finally understood the pantomime and her hand frantically shot up and reached her hairpiece just as it was dangling from her head. She adjusted it into an even more ridiculous looking position.

"Serena, is it true that you are the famous mermaid the entire world has been searching for?"

The camera moved to Serena and the makeup man took the opportunity to run on stage and batten down Cynthia's wig. Serena's beautiful face filled the screen but she was so mesmerized by Cynthia's hair falling off she couldn't speak. Never before had she seen hair that came off. Cynthia's hair was reattached, but she noticed her guest was not answering her question. She was just staring at her wig.

"Uh, Serena," Cynthia repositioned herself as the camera pulled back to include her in the shot, "do you actually have fins when you are in water?"

Serena's mouth was opened as she continued to stare at the mop of hair on Cynthia's head. Cynthia was feeling a blush run through her body that started at her toes and ran up to the top of her head.

"Captain Corbin, maybe you can help us here. Isn't it true that you brought Serena here to appeal to the president and the military to stop detonating atomic weapons in the Pacific Ocean, the supposed home of Serena and her people?" Cynthia relaxed a bit when Corbin jumped in. But Serena was still staring sideways at Cynthia's wig.

"Yes, the bombs have caused serious disturbances to the ocean floor, causing seaquakes along with radiation sickness and widespread famine."

"Isn't it true that you spent the last ten years living among these so-called MerPeople?"

Cynthia was just starting to feel at ease when Serena reached her hand out and jerked the wig off Cynthia's head. She held it in her hand, combing her fingers through it. Cynthia tried to compose herself but she looked like she had just been goosed.

Corbin tried his best to ignore Serena. "Yes. Uhh, myself and two fellow officers had an opportunity to observe and study them."

Back in the luxury of the hotel suite, Doc was kicked back on the sofa watching Serena on TV and laughing his ass off. "You little siren!"

"And what are these people like, Captain?" Cynthia was also trying her best to ignore Serena.

"This is very nice, may I keep it?" Serena asked.

Cynthia shook her head nervously. Serena smiled and plopped it on her head, covering her eyes, then peeked out from behind it and giggled.

Corbin folded his hands and looked at Serena. "They are very playful, mischievous creatures..." Corbin broke into a snicker as he looked at Serena peeking through the hairpiece. He suddenly felt a lump in his throat and his heart went all fuzzy. "A simple, kind and uncomplicated species who want nothing more than to be left alone to live out their lives in peace and harmony in their God given home...Mother Ocean."

Serena lowered the wig. She looked into Corbin's eyes and smiled a sincere smile. Tears welled up in her eyes. She swallowed hard and looked straight into the camera. With great dignity and intensity in her eyes she said, "You Landers have been encroaching on our world for centuries but what you don't realize is that if our oceans die, you Landers will also die. I don't know how you got the idea that everything you see belongs to you and you can do with it as you please. But you can't. Sooner or later you will pay for your governments' actions. And if you don't try and stop them you are just as responsible!"

Serena handed the tuft of hair back to Cynthia, who looked

down at it. "It's time to start listening to Mother Ocean and start respecting her and her creatures!"

Cynthia held the floating tufts of hair in her hand as she tried her best to maintain a stoic newscaster composure. "And that's the news this morning from our nation's capital." Cynthia smiled, but it was forced and contrived. "I'm Cynthia Brinkle, thanks for joining us."

"And cut," the director screamed, out of breath. He was beside himself.

Cynthia jumped up and ran off the set. "I've never been so humiliated in all my life."

Corbin leaned over and kissed Serena.

"You're not angry?" Serena looked up faintly and smiled. Corbin shook his head no.

Serena smiled weakly, then collapsed into Corbin's arms.

All morning NBC had been swamped with phone calls and telegrams wanting to know more about the "Mermaid in Washington." By noon Serena had started a movement. By the evening people were picketing the White House carrying signs that read: Save the Whales; Save the MerPeople; Save Mother Ocean; and Stop Atomic Weapons Testing NOW!

Cynthia Brinkle, who swore she would never be caught dead in the same room with that mermaid, found herself on the phone begging Corbin for a second interview.

Corbin stared out the window at the Washington Monument. He could hear the picketers from his open hotel window. "I'm sorry Miss Brinkle, Serena isn't doing any more interviews." Corbin listened patiently as the woman railed on at the other end of the phone line. "Absolutely not! At the moment she has more pressing concerns."

Cynthia was sitting in her office. The White House was visible in the background. "What could possibly be more pressing than the welfare of the planet?" Cynthia turned on her reporter charm. "Captain Corbin, surely you see that Serena is key to the survival of our oceans. If those warmongers keep polluting our oceans, well," she stumbled for her words, wishing she had a fresh copy in front of her, "how long do you think we will last...without...uh...Mother Ocean? Ninety percent of our oxygen supply comes from the ocean..." Cynthia was feeling very smug quoting her most recent research when she heard the click of Corbin disconnecting the phone.

"Damn, he's taken her over to CBS, I just know it!"

Corbin walked into the bathroom and looked into Doc's grave face and then down at Serena, who silently lay on the bottom of the bathtub. She was very pale and struggled to lift her head.

"Tell us what to do for you." Corbin picked up her hand. Tears rolled down his check. "Serena, I can't lose you."

Serena smiled faintly at Corbin. The phone rang again. Doc patted Corbin on the back and left to answer the phone. He poked his head back in the bathroom and whispered, "Top brass on the line." Doc's voice jerked Corbin back to his senses.

Corbin wiped his tears away as he walked angrily toward the phone. *Goddamn it! Why couldn't they just leave her alone? What did she or any of her people ever do to anyone?* Corbin thought as he gazed toward the bathroom, finally realizing Serena's body wasn't made for his Lander World. He had to get her back to MerWorld. He knew she may not make it and he didn't want her death to be for nothing.

"Corbin, how dare you take her public!" Greer yelled.

"Look, Greer, you know what we want. Just do it and we'll shut up!" Corbin slammed down the phone.

Greer paced up and down in his office. The carpet was a thick forest green and the walls were paneled in ash wood. "I'll be damned if a mermaid is going to get in my way." He picked up the phone. "Winston!" Greer hollered, "Get that newswoman on the horn!"

"Cynthia Brinkle?" Winston's eyes lit up.

"Yeah, the bitch who interviewed Corbin, and after that, track down my grandson."

Cynthia was still trying to find out who had stolen her story when Greer's phone call came in.

"If it wasn't CBS then who was it?" Cynthia fumbled through her Rolodex. "Damn, who's got her now?"

"Cindy, there's an admiral on the phone for you," a fellow newscaster interrupted her.

Cynthia buried her head in her hands. "Can't you see I'm busy! Wait! Did you say an admiral?"

"He wants to talk to you." The man held his hand over the receiver. "You'd better pick up, I think he's important."

Cynthia plastered on a fake smile and picked up the phone. "Hello General, I mean Admiral, this is Cynthia Brinkle, how can I help you?" Cynthia's expression turned from annoyed to inquisitive and finally to excited... "You don't say, well, of course...anything to serve my country. Sir...you did say I would have an exclusive? I'll air it on tonight's news! Yes, sir, and thank you, sir." Cynthia hung up the phone and smiled an evil smirk.

Serena sat on the sofa in the living room of the hotel suite. She was wrapped in a blanket and Doc held Serena's head while she convulsed. Corbin stood by feeling helpless. Rachel's face passed before him. Corbin remembered trying to stop the blood. He rubbed his hands over his face and thought about the irony of it all. Rachel had died at sea and Serena was dying on land.

His eyes were filled with tears as he knelt beside her and took her hand. *Why am I always losing the ones I love most?* "Serena, I can't lose you!"

Serena's smile faded and she closed her eyes. A loud knock at the door shook Corbin back into reality.

"I'll get rid of them." Corbin walked over and opened the door.

"I think you'd better have a look at the news, sir." John rushed into the room and over to the TV. He turned it on. Corbin noticed the words "Mermaid Fraud" written over a photo of Serena's face. The well-coiffed and perfectly made-up face of Cynthia Brinkle filled the screen. She stared smugly into the camera.

"Here's the latest development in our story about Serena the Mermaid Queen who supposedly came to Washington to stop the military from killing her MerPeople under the Pacific Ocean. It turns out that there may be something fishy about Serena's tale. A picture of Serena wearing a Russian hat flashed onscreen. "It turns out our little mermaid may not be telling the truth." Cynthia stared pointblank into the camera. Her smile turned into a smirk.

"What in the hell is this crap!" Corbin couldn't contain his temper.

"Shush." John quieted him.

"The woman who claimed to be a mermaid and a representative of an ancient underwater civilization is now thought to be a Russian spy. Her plea before the president of the United States to stop destroying the oceans is now thought to be a ploy from the communist government to weaken our country's defense structure. We have Admiral Nathan Greer here to comment on this."

"That son of a bitch!" Corbin hit the wall. "I tell you, John, your Grandpa doesn't miss a trick!"

"Our intelligence informs us that the man reported to be Captain James Corbin of the USS *Poseidon* and Serena, the self-professed mermaid, are in fact double agents."

"Double agents my ass!" Corbin railed.

"Admiral, this hits pretty close to home for you, sir? I mean, Captain Corbin was married to your late daughter."

"That's correct, which makes this even harder to swallow. Unfortunately we have the documentation that Corbin turned traitor during the war and was in fact working with the Japanese during the time period he claimed to have been living under the sea in this so-called MerWorld. After the war he went to Russia." A picture of Corbin in the same stupid Russian hat flashed on the television screen.

"Oh God!" Corbin groaned.

"Where he met Serena, alias Natasha Kilvichakoff."

"Natasha Kilvichakoff?" Doc smiled. "Now that has a ring to it. By the way, I really like you in that hat." Doc winked at Corbin, then turned off the television.

"Needless to say, we've got to get you and her out of here. Can she travel?" John looked at Serena.

"Come on baby!" Corbin leaned over and picked Serena up in his arms. "We have to get a move on."

Serena laid her head against Corbin's chest.

"I've located your old submarine, it's in New London. I think they want to make it into a museum piece."

"A museum piece!" Doc snorted.

"Well it is the only sub in the navy with a golden ass!" Corbin held Serena tightly.

"I made a deal with the guy in charge of security. Everything's set." John looked around the room for an alternate way out.

Serena let out a painful squeal.

Corbin ran his hand through her hair. "I know, I know, but our only hope is to get you back, honey." Corbin looked down at Serena. "We've got to risk it, but I can't ask you two to ruin your careers."

"I'm still waiting for my back pay." Doc sighed, "I guess I'll never see it."

"I don't mind helping out, it's the least I can do for my old man." John smiled but the warmth was not there. The phone rang. Both John and Corbin stared at it.

"Don't answer it!" John cried out.

Corbin slowly picked it up and held the receiver to his ear and listened.

"I leave you two alone for a few days and see what a fine mess you get yourselves into!" Pots's voice rang out on the other end of the line.

"Pots you ol' son of a bitch! It's good to hear your voice! How the hell are you?" Corbin was still holding Serena.

Pots was standing in the living room of a rundown house. Encircling him were twelve family members. A big fat woman who looked a lot like Pots was screaming at the top of her lungs. He covered his ear. "Oh great, everything is just great!" Five toddlers ran around the tiny room. The great woman slapped one of them on its behind as they ran past.

Corbin listened. "Are you sure everything's all right?"

Pots covered the phone. "Would you all SHUT UP for one minute, Good Lord, can't a man have a moment's peace!" His entire family froze and stared at him.

"Ungrateful," someone murmured under their breath.

Pots sighed with relief. "How's Serena?" Pots's voice showed concern.

"Not so great." Corbin looked up at John who pointed impatiently to his watch. Corbin nodded. "In fact, John's here and we're going to see if we can get the old heap out of hock and take her on a sightseeing tour of the Pacific."

"Where is the ol' *Poseidon* anyway?" Pots whispered into the phone.

"It's in New London, get this, they want to make a museum piece out of it." Corbin mustered up a laugh.

"Well, it is the only sub I know with a golden ass!" Pots laughed.

"That's what I said. Well, I've got to go, Pots, so long old buddy." Corbin hung up the phone.

"Okay, let's do it." Corbin looked at John.

CHAPTER TWENTY-FIVE

"We traveled the back roads from Washington, D.C. to New London, Connecticut in an old beat up truck John had managed to get his hands on. I was too sick to even move. Corbin held me the whole way. When we arrived in New London, Pots was there to greet us. I guess he had his fill of Lander life too.

We passed through security at New London, boarded Corbin's ship and slipped out to sea, virtually undetected. At the time I didn't think anything of it. I was too sick to sense that things were happening too easily."

"Her blood pressure is dropping," Corbin cried out. He sat next to Serena on the coffin rack.

"Do something Doc!"

Doc listened to her heart with his stethoscope. "We're losing her!"

Corbin squeezed Serena's hand. "Serena, stay with me!"

"Look out!!! Coming though! COMING THROUGH!" Pots pushed his way into the tiny compartment. He wielded a huge pot.

"Stand aside." He pushed Doc and Corbin aside and poured the pot of water over Serena.

"What in the hell!" Corbin looked up at Pots. Serena opened her eyes. Doc listened to her heart and smiled. "She's back! We've got her back!" Doc beamed.

"Pots, thank you!" Corbin smiled.

"Nothing that a little fresh seawater can't cure!" Pots laughed and took the pot back to the galley.

"May I come in?" John stood at the door of the compartment.

"Sure!" Corbin smiled as Serena opened her eyes and looked at John.

"She looks like she's doing better." John looked down at Serena; his eyes were cold.

"Yeah, she's doing okay." Corbin smiled at Serena and squeezed her hand.

"Sir, may I have a word with you?" John's demeanor was quite formal.

"I'll be right back." Corbin's hand trailed Serena's arm and finally their fingers parted. Serena watched Corbin walk away with John. Concern filled her eyes.

"How long will it take for us to arrive at MerWorld?" John fidgeted with a pen he held in his hands.

"Two or three weeks if our fuel holds out. Why?" Corbin looked John in the eye.

"I don't think we should go through the Panama Canal, I'm sure Greer will have them looking for us there."

"Yeah," Corbin nodded. "That means we'll have to go under the ice. Damn I was hoping to let Serena out for a swim when we hit the warm Caribbean waters."

"Greer's sure to be on our tail, we can't waste time." John pressed hard upon his father.

Corbin rubbed the back of his neck. "It's a tough call, but I suppose you're right."

"Corbin was enjoying being back in command of the USS *Poseidon*. We headed up toward Antarctica and passed under the huge glaciers. Pots boiled buckets of seawater and Doc and Corbin took turns giving me saltwater baths."

Serena lay in Corbin's bunk. She squealed in Dolphin.

"We're breaking through the ice and we should reach the warm French Polynesian Islands in a few days, then on to your home waters." Corbin looked into Serena's crystal blue eyes.

She tried to squeal, but all that came out was a weird kind of sonar sound. Corbin sympathetically smiled.

"My poor little Dolphin girl has lost her squeal." Corbin kissed her cheek. She smiled and stuck out her tongue playfully.

"You'd better watch out or you might get more than you bargained for." Corbin kissed Serena's ear. Her body wriggled with pleasure. He placed his hand over her breast and ran it inside her shirt, opening it and exposing her bare breasts. He teased his mouth over her nipples and delicately titillated them with his tongue. Her body responded to his touch as she found her squeal again and used it to show her pleasure.

"Now there's the squeal I know and love!" Corbin pulled the pocket door shut. The quarters were close but Corbin knew how to maneuver in confined spaces. He took off his shirt and undid his pants while running his tongue over her nipples. Serena's squeals grew with her passion. Corbin jumped up into the bunk, hitting his head.

"Ouch! Goddammit!"

Serena laughed. "Don't worry, I'm not going anywhere."

Corbin lunged on top of her. "Not if I can help it." He looked into her eyes. "God, I missed doing this with you."

"Doing what?" Serena looked up, feigning naivety.

"This." Corbin kissed her deeply. He pulled back and looked into Serena's deep crystal blue eyes. His hands groped her body, moving first over her soft round breasts, then down between her muscular, slimy legs. He massaged her tube suckers between her legs and slipped his fingers into her. Serena's body buckled and swayed with the rhythm of Corbin's thrusts.

Doc pushed himself through the sub's narrow hallway. He was outside Corbin's cabin when he heard Serena squeal. Alarm crossed his face. Then he heard a moan. It was clearly not a painful moan. He smiled and rubbed his chin, then proceeded on down the hall.

"Glad to see my patient's recovered!" Doc bellowed as he climbed past the doorway.

Corbin and Serena stopped what they were doing and looked at each other, then giggled.

"Let's get back to your therapy." Corbin kissed Serena, slipping himself inside her. Serena gave herself over to Corbin totally and completely. Each thrust became more desperate as he realized, by almost losing her, how much he loved her. This mysterious mermaid that never seemed to be completely his. He had wanted her forever, and now that he had her, he could never bear to lose her again.

Serena, too, wanted to be one with this Lander. To merge with him dissolving all boundaries that separated them, making their bodies, minds and spirits one. Serena climaxed first with a loud cry, then Corbin followed. There was no separation, no division, they were one! They melted into one another's arms, clinging to the moment, riding the wave of ecstasy, and trying to hold onto the moment forever before facing something that may tear them apart.

"The next day we broke through the ice and in two days we were closing in on MerWorld. My spirits soared and so did my powers. I knew then my dreams of living a Lander life with Corbin could never be realized, but I was prepared to give it all up if I could just stay with him. I had been happy for a few brief moments in his world, but now I had to return to warn my people and, if needed, lead them back home."

Corbin was topside in the control room watching the seas for signs of MerWorld while Serena, who was feeling much better, walked into the galley. John sat drinking a cup of coffee.

"Good morning." Serena smiled. John looked down into his cup.

Serena sat down beside John. "You don't like me very much, do you?"

John looked up, shocked by her candidness.

"Is it because you think I stole your father's love?" Serena wasn't one to make small talk.

"I don't know what you are talking about." John hunched over his cup. Honesty was not part of his upbringing.

Serena scooted closer to him. "Why don't you ever wear your necklace out?"

"What necklace?" John looked defensive.

"The necklace you have hidden under your shirt." Serena teased, "Is it because you think it looks too feminine?"

"How do you know about that?" John looked shocked.

"Because I gave it to you." Serena smiled.

"That's a lie! It was my mother's." John put his hand over his shirt defensively.

"You know, it has special powers. The broken heart can heal a wounded heart, if you let it," Serena whispered gently.

John pulled away. "How did you know it was a broken heart?"

"Your father didn't kill your mother like your grandfather told you. He's a captain and naturally he takes on too much responsibility. He always blames himself for everything that happens around him. He loved your mother."

John's body began to shake. "How do you know these things?" His eyes flashed angry.

"I know because I was there." Serena gently reached out, trying to open his shirt to touch the necklace. John jerked back.

"Maybe you aren't really angry at your father. Maybe you're really angry at yourself. That's why you've been making yourself sick, going out on all those dives."

John swallowed hard. He pressed his hand against his cheek and sighed deeply. He wanted to say it wasn't true. He wanted to call her a liar...but he just stared down at the coffee grinds in the bottom of his cup.

"It's time you stopped blaming yourself."

John squeezed the mug so tight he thought it would break in his hands.

"It wasn't your fault! Your mother died. She just died. That's all there is to it."

A tear rolled down John's cheek.

Serena spoke gently, "It happens. I know. A mother's love is a precious thing but we can't always have it." Serena wiped the tear from his cheek. "Besides, wouldn't she want you two to love and care for each other?" Serena tasted the tears on her finger and smiled. "Salty, like Mother Ocean."

She smiled and looked at him with a piercing gaze. "When I saw you lying there next to your mother's body I knew the pain you would face growing up alone. That was the necklace my mother left me. It helped me to grow up and I hope it helped you." Serena touched his face gently. Shocked, John let her hold his cheek for a moment.

"It did. Thank you." John pulled the necklace from around his neck.

"I think it's time this necklace found its way back to you." John took the necklace from his neck and placed it in Serena's hand.

She looked at it contemplatively. "Maybe you're right." She took her broken heart from inside her shirt. She connected the two halves to form a whole. It was as if a ripple of healing energy emanated forth from the two joined halves that had once again found each other. It filled the whole ocean.

"MERWORLD HO!" Pots ran into the galley.

Serena let out a squeal of delight and ran toward the conning tower.

Greer! John thought to himself. *I've got to warn them!* John followed Serena up the ladder into the conning tower.

"John, over here." Corbin put his arm around his son.

"Dad, I, I..." John was interrupted by Doc.

"Captain, I'm picking up something on the sonar!"

Doc, Corbin and Serena stared at the screen.

"What in the hell is that?" Corbin shouted.

"It's Greer." John looked into his father's eyes.

"How would you know that?" Corbin stared back.

"Because he's following a homing device I planted on the sub," John responded.

"Good God, what have you done, son?" Corbin looked at the sonar screen.

"He's closing in, sir." Doc watched the beep on the sonar.

"What exactly is that?" Corbin stared at the bleep on screen.

"It's called the Polaris; it's a prototype nuclear sub. On board is a nuclear warhead that makes Hiroshima look like a birthday candle." John's voice was flat.

Serena pressed between the two men and looked at the screen, then looked at Corbin. "Great Mother of Whales!"

Corbin looked at Serena, then at John. "How could you do this?"

John backed away but Corbin kept coming. Corbin lunged and put his fingers around John's throat.

John coughed. "He poisoned me. He poisoned my mind against you with stories about how you killed my mother and he poisoned my body...and you weren't there to STOP HIM!" John sobbed.

Corbin looked down at his hands wrapped around his son's neck as he cried. Doc rushed over and put a gentle hand on Corbin's back and whispered in his ear, "Corbin, he's your son."

All at once it was little frightened Johnnie, the infant he had abandoned. The child he had left all alone to face Greer. Corbin loosened his hands around his son's neck and embraced him.

"I'm sorry John." Corbin cried as he held his son tight, "I'm sorry I wasn't there for you."

The two men lay on the floor of the sub, crying in each other's arms, when all at once an ungodly sound shattered the silence. It was the sound of metal grating against rock. The sub shook.

"She's ramming against the cave wall!" Doc replied.

Corbin helped his son up.

Doc looked over Serena's shoulder. "It's going to be tight!"

Corbin stared at John as he shouted orders to Pots, "Full speed ahead. Hold on everyone!"

The grating sound continued. Doc tore off his headphones. Everyone covered their ears. The noise sounded like the hull was being ripped in two.

"She can't take much more of this." Doc held onto a pipe as the sub shook. Water burst forth from it, knocking Doc down. John and Corbin struggled to close off the pipes.

Water was spilling everywhere as the horrible grating noise almost burst their eardrums. Serena closed her eyes and let out a beautiful sound. Suddenly the grating noise stopped, and the sub stopped shaking and stabilized.

"We're through!" Doc put on his headphones. "But we're taking on too much water. We're going down."

"Let's try and reach the city!" Corbin looked at the screen. "Full speed ahead!" Corbin shouted as he broke open the case that held the firearms. "Needless to say this isn't going to be an underwater tea party."

"Come on sweetheart, don't quit on me now," Doc coached the ol' *Poseidon*.

The sub cut through the main dome just as it had ten years before, only this time Corbin was prepared. He was armed and ready. The sub came to a full stop. Half of the sub was inside the bubble and the other half jutted out. The bubble wall closed around it. Inside, the small party stood silently looking at the hatch.

Corbin grabbed his gun and stuck it into his pants. He turned to Serena and gave her a kiss. "You all stay here and let me receive the warm welcome."

Corbin climbed up the ladder and made a full turn. With another turn, the hatch opened and he stuck his head out but was immediately lifted up and thrown down onto the deck of the sub by Jaween, who towered over him. Serena climbed out of the hatch next. She squealed out in Dolphin, trying to reason with Jaween, but he turned with his hand ready to strike her across the face.

Corbin managed to squeeze the trigger of his gun and a bullet hit Jaween's shoulder. He took aim to fire again but Jaween lunged on top of him and the gun fell from his fingers. Jaween raised his hand again, ready to strike a deadly blow, when a bullet hit him in his back. Jaween turned in surprise to find Serena holding the gun. He lunged toward her but she fired again, piercing him through his heart. Jaween's horrid mouth opened wide, dark ink oozed out and his black shark eyes rolled back into his head. He dropped dead on the ocean floor.

Serena dropped the gun. "He was my brother."

Corbin stood up and took Serena in his arms.

A low murmur spread throughout the Quams. It started out low, then picked up in strength, *"Kilahara, Kilahara, Kilahara."* It rose to a deafening level.

John climbed out from the sub, followed by Doc, then Pots. John stood still, awed by the amazing sight: the splendid dome structure and the myriad of bubbles strung together creating the magnificent city. He looked around at the thousands of MerPeople chanting *Kilahara* and pointing to his father.

Pots whispered to Doc, "Are they still chanting that *Kilahara* crap?"

"Some things never change." Doc smiled. "Ah, but it's good to be home." Doc stepped over Jaween's dead carcass. "I see they've made a few improvements around the place."

"Don't they have anything better to do?" Pots murmured as he searched the crowd for Oceania.

Marianna was the first to break through the huddled mob

of MerPeople. She grabbed hold of Doc, then Oceania ran up to Pots and enveloped him in her arms.

"I told you I'd be back, baby." Pots kissed Oceania.

"Did you miss me?" Doc looked into Marianna's moist sea green eyes.

John's mouth was still wide open in awe.

"Sorry to ruin this magic moment, but your beeper is blinking." Doc tapped John on the shoulder.

John looked down. "Damn, it's Greer. He's headed for the city." John looked at a blinking light outside the bubbled city. "He's got a nuclear warhead strapped to the CUV."

The crowd stopped chanting and looked at the approaching light.

"I must get my people to safety." Serena looked over at Marianna and Oceania, who embraced her. Tears flowed as the three MerWomen held each other. A TurtleBoy ran up holding Serena's crown. Marianna picked up the crown.

"You are our ruler now. Tell us what we must do."

"As Marianna placed the crown on my head I once again felt an immense vibration surge through my body. I opened my mouth, giving forth the most beautiful Whale Song. This time there was no one to stop me. The incredible sound grew and was carried throughout the waters, inundating the city with its electromagnetic force. Quam members, young and old alike, felt summoned by the vibration. It was as though the song stirred some ancient memory that had lain dormant deep inside them and was now awakened. They listened not only with their ears, but with their soul. It was as if something encoded in their DNA had been waiting all this time to be freed by this sound. Like some pre-choreographed dance, MerMen, MerWomen and MerChildren began evacuating the city by the hundreds."

"Hurry! You've got to get out of here!" John cried as he watched Greer's CUV coming toward them.

Corbin turned to Serena. "Go ahead Serena, lead your

people to safety." He looked over at Doc and Pots. "Go on ahead."

Tears filled Serena's eyes. She buried her face against Corbin's neck and whispered into his ear, "I can't leave you!"

Corbin smiled tenderly. He knew the pain she felt because he had felt the same when he faced the possibility of losing her.

He turned to John. Corbin laid his hand on his son's shoulder. "I can't leave you, son."

"It's all right Dad, you came back for me. That's what counts." John threw his arms around his father and pulled him close. "Please Dad." He whispered into his father's ear, "You and I both know I'm dead already."

Corbin let out a long, hard sigh and shook his head, then he grabbed his son around the neck.

"I love you son." Tears filled Corbin's eyes.

"I love you too, Dad." John pushed back.

Corbin took Serena's hand. "All right, we'll give it a try."

Corbin stepped into a transport bubble. Doc and Pots had already left the cave in the massive exodus of MerPeople with Oceania and Marianna pushing their protective bubble encasement.

Corbin looked back at John as Serena pushed his bubble through the wall. John watched the MerPeople heading out the cave exit, then he climbed inside the sub to wait for Greer.

Greer watched from inside the CUV.

"They're all leaving, Goddammit! Where the hell are they going?" Greer hollered at the technician piloting the CUV. "Turn this thing around!"

"I can't sir!" The pilot fidgeted with his control panel. "We hit some rubble on the way in and the CUV is inoperable. I can't control it!"

Greer watched as Mermaids swam by holding their MerChildren protectively in their arms. None of the Shark

Quam had followed Serena. They had been virtually unaffected by Serena's Whale Song. Instead they just stared in confusion at their leader's lifeless body.

Greer's CUV slid through the bubble and crash landed on the floor of the Amphitheater right beside the sub. He nudged the lifeless body of the pilot that was flopped over the control panel. Greer climbed out of the CUV and looked at the warhead. The timer was flashing. It read six minutes. He fidgeted with the controls but they were jammed. He hit the timer out of frustration but it just kept ticking away. At that moment he observed the hatch slowly unscrew.

Greer smiled, "At least I'm taking your sorry ass with me, Corbin!" Greer watched as John climbed out of the sub instead.

"He's gone," John yelled out.

"GONE? Why did you let him go!" Greer yelled out in anger.

John slowly climbed down from the deck and walked over to Greer. He stared straight into his eyes, something he had never had the courage to do in all the days of his life.

"All those years, I believed in you, I did whatever you asked, never thinking about myself or what I wanted...everything was for you, you and your navy!"

Greer started to interrupt but John silenced him with his intense stare.

"I never even stopped to ask if what you were doing was right. I'd have done whatever you asked even if it killed me." John let loose a laugh. "And it has killed me! Now the only pleasure I have left is in knowing that I'm taking you with me. There will be one less self-centered, power-hungry bastard on this planet making life miserable for the rest of us. And in knowing that the truth will not die with me."

Greer was in shock. He couldn't believe the words his grandson was uttering.

"That's right, grandfather. Kate stole your coveted secret files and gave them to me. I made copies and left them with my girlfriend, Admiral Pruett's daughter. So at last the world will know what you and your navy have done to this race of MerPeople. They will all know what a bastard you really are!"

Greer was so surprised at finally seeing his grandson stand up to him that he had forgotten all about the bomb. The timer clicked zero. A huge explosion reverberated throughout the ocean. The underwater cave was blown open. The Polaris prototype sub was caught in the huge wake and tumbled over several times.

"All of the Quam members had managed to swim far away from the blast. They were safely on their way toward the Portal of Time. My Whale Song had been a signal to them that our time on this planet was finished and it was time to return home.

I, however, was desperately pushing Corbin toward safety when the bomb exploded. The wake hit with such a powerful force that it burst Corbin's bubble. I embraced him and we looked up at the many fathoms of water separating us from the surface. I knew Corbin would never make it. He smiled at me and I held him tightly. I was still frantically trying to figure some way to save him. He gently took my face into his hands and mouthed the words: *I love you*.

Corbin's powerful body clutched mine. I felt the pounding of his heart and the tickle of his whiskers against my cheek, shooting chills down the back of my neck. Our intertwined bodies drifted in the vast turquoise sea. Corbin, sensing my fear and desperation, and hoping to ease my despair, kissed me deeply and passionately with his last breath. I felt my nipples harden as waves of excitement ripped through my body. I ached to have him inside me. I pressed my lips hard against his, hoping to give him the *Kiss of Life*! His pulse raced with excitement, then, in one moment, he was gone. Silence echoed throughout the water. I felt the warmth leaving his body. I grabbed hold of his limp hands and pulled his hardening lips away from my mouth. I stared into his eyes, searching for him, but they were empty. His soul was gone. A spray of bubbles escaped from my mouth and rose to the surface, laden with my anguish. I pushed Corbin's body away, refusing the reality of the moment as I clutched the Emerald Heart that hung between my breasts. Pain surged through my body. *Oh Great Whale Mother, help me!* I cried as I watched Corbin's lifeless body sink into the depths of the Abyss, never to touch me again.

I didn't care about my people; I didn't care about the Whale Women. All I wanted was to be with Corbin. I had spent all this time worrying about MerWorld, and now that Corbin was gone, I realized that he was the most important thing in my life. It was too much for me to bear. I too wanted to die. I had nothing left to live for. I had tried to give him the *Kiss of Life*, but my love had not been strong enough to create the change. I drew all the inner strength from the depths of my soul, from my seasons of Whale Woman training, and from my love of Mother Ocean. I swam toward the Abyss to see my people safely to the other side. It was my last duty of this world, then I too would go to the other side as my mother and father had before me. I would return to the world from whence I came. That was my only consolation.

As I swam toward the glowing Portal I prepared myself for the transition. I was ready. There was nothing left to tie me to this wayward planet. As I watched the last of my people pass through the Portal of Time, I beat my tail against the currents and flung myself toward the Portal, but to my surprise it closed in front of me. The bright vortex was now clear. I saw the face of my mother, Chaila, and my father, Triton. I felt a great sadness at not being able to pass through.

I heard my mother's voice in my mind. *No, my dearest daughter, your job is not yet finished.* I wanted to push myself through the Portal. I was finished with this world! I wanted to return home. *The one you love lives and you must rejoin him in another time, another place. Go now.*

Her words haunted my mind.

The two images faded and the lights dimmed; I was left alone in the darkness. Was it true? Did Corbin live? Were we to be reunited? Impossible...unless the *Kiss of Life* had worked its miracle. But how would I find him? I felt my body being churned about. I was hurled upwards at an astounding rate and found myself spat out into the ocean's surface waters, but what ocean? It all looked so unfamiliar. I was confused. I was in another place, and yes, it felt distinctly like a different time.

Was it the past...was it the future? All I knew was that my love
was still alive and I had to find him.

The Cosmic Sea of Love

Come with me, my love, to the cosmic Sea of Love.
Where we'll pass away our time in sensual pleasure and delight,
Where a watery grave awaits you if your true love is not right.
Follow me, O mortal man, to the depths of the ocean floor
And gaze upon your family, friends, and comrades never more.
Follow me so swiftly as you disappear down below
And hear your name called gently
In the summer breeze that blows.
Leave behind your Lander cares and surrender to the sea
For you and I shall share a love
That will bind you eternally to me.

9 781958 184295